THE SEVEN MYSTERIES.

MYSTERY I.—THE STONE-CUTTER OF MONTROUGE.

The Stone-cutter.—*Page 5.*

TO MR. ————

MY DEAR FRIEND,—You have frequently said to me at those pleasant meetings, which are now become so rare, where each one talks at leisure, and either tells some dream of his heart, following the first caprice of his imagination, or runs through the treasure of his reminiscences—you have frequently said to me, that since the days of Scheherazade and after Nodier, I was one of the most amusing tale-tellers you had ever listened to.

Therefore you wrote to me to-day to say, that while awaiting a long romance from my pen—one of those interminable romances, you know, such as I sometimes write, and in which I introduce a whole century,—you wished to have a few tales,—two, four, or six volumes at the utmost, poor flowers of my garden, which you intended to throw among the political preoccupations of the moment; between the trial at Bourges, for example, and the elections in May.

Alas! my friend, these are gloomy days, and my tales, let me inform you, will not be gay ones. Only, you must permit me, wearied and disgusted by all which I see passing around me in real life, to draw my subjects from the realms of imagination. Alas! I much fear that all the most elevated, the most visionary, the most poetical spirits, are at this moment where mine is also, wandering through the ideal world, the only refuge which Heaven has left us from cold stern reality.

I am at this moment surrounded by at least fifty open volumes, which I am consulting while writing a history of the Regency, which I have almost finished, and which I beg you will warn mothers, if you think of it, not to allow their daughters to read. Well! as I said before, such is my present occupation, and while I am writing to you, my eyes fall upon a passage in the memoirs of the Marquis d'Argenson, where, under this heading: "*On Conversation, past and present,*" I read as follows:

"I am convinced that during the period when the Hôtel Rambouillet gave the tone to high society, they listened well and they argued better: they cultivated taste and spirit. I have myself seen a few models of that species of conversation among the old persons who were at court when I was. Their conversation was energetic and refined; they always used the proper word in the proper place; sometimes antithetically, it is true, but in such a manner that every sentence augmented the sense of the subject; they were learned without being pedantic, gay without being malicious."

It is exactly a hundred years ago since the Marquis d'Argenson wrote these lines, which I have copied from his book. He was, at the period when he wrote them, nearly of the same age as we now are; and, like him, my dear friend, we can say: "We have known men of the old school, who were, alas! what we no longer are, that is, men of polished manners and high breeding."

We may have seen them, but our sons will not. Therefore, although we are not worth much, we are worth more than our sons will be.

It is true that every day we make a step towards "liberty, equality, and fraternity," the three great words which the Revolution of '93, and more recently its daughter, that of 1848, has thrown into the midst of modern society, as she would have done at a tiger, a lion, or a bear, clothed in lambs' fleeces; empty words, unfortunately, and which can be read through the smoke of June written with shot on our public monuments.

As for me, I go with the stream; I follow the general movement. God forbid that I should preach "Stand still!"—for such a doctrine is stagnation, death. But I go on like one of those men of whom Dante speaks—whose feet move forward, it is true, but whose heads are turned in the same direction as their heels.

And that which I look for in vain—that which I regret the most—that which my retrospective glance finds only among the things which are gone, is the society which is disappearing, evaporating, vanishing away like one of those phantoms whose history I am about to tell you.

And this society, so elegant, so courteous, so refined, which constituted that life which was worth the trouble of *living* (if I may be allowed the expression), has it been long dead, or have we killed it?

Ah! I remember when quite a child that my father took me to visit Madame de Montesson. She was a very grand lady, a woman of another century altogether. She had married the Duke d'Orleans, the grandfather of king Louis Philippe, nearly sixty years before; she was then ninety years of age. She lived in a magnificent great hotel in the Chaussée d'Antin. Napoleon gave her an annuity of a hundred thousand crowns. Do you know for what reason she was entitled to this pension?—in what manner it was inscribed in the red book of Louis the Sixteenth's successor?—No!—Well! Madame de Montesson received from the Emperor an annuity of a hundred thousand crowns *for having preserved in her saloons the traditions of high society of the times of Louis XIV. and Louis XV.*

That is exactly half the sum which the Chamber of Deputies now gives to his nephew that he may make France forget that which his uncle wished her to remember!

You will scarcely believe one thing, my dear friend, and that is, that the two words which I have just had the imprudence to mention—*the Chamber*—bring me back direct to the memoirs of the Marquis d'Argenson.

How so?

You shall see.

"They complain," he goes on to say, "that in our days the art of conversation is no longer understood in France. I can easily divine the reason. It is because the patience to listen diminishes every day among our contemporaries. They listen badly, or far more frequently, they will not listen at all. I have remarked this even in the best society which I frequent."

Now, my dear friend, which is the best society which we can frequent in our days? It is undeniably that which the eight million electors have judged worthy to represent the interests, the opinions, and the talents of France. In fact, it is the Chamber of Deputies.

Well, enter the Chamber of Deputies at any hour of the day when you may chance to be passing. I will wager a hundred to one, that you will find one of the deputies in the tribune speaking, and upon the seats from four or five hundred persons who are not listening to him but interrupting him every minute.

This is so notorious a fact, that one of the articles of the Constitution of 1848, expressly forbids all interruptions.

Then count all the whispers and rappings of the knuckles given in the Chamber during the year or thereabouts since it assembled:—they are innumerable!

Always, be it understood, in the name of "liberty, fraternity, equality" too!

Therefore, my dear friend, as I have already told you, I regret a great many things, it is not so? although I have scarcely attained half the ordinary average of human existence. Well! that which I regret the most, after all, is that which the Marquis d'Argenson regretted a hundred years ago—*courtesy.*

And yet in the days of the Marquis d'Argenson, such an idea had never entered their heads as to call one another *citizen*—think of that.

Suppose some one had said to the Marquis d'Argenson at the period when he was writing these memoirs, for instance :

"See what we have come to in France now-a-days : the curtain falls ; the scene closes, there is nothing left but whistles and cat-calls. Soon we shall have no elegant tale-tellers in society, no arts, no pictures, no palaces built ; but envy, here, there, and everywhere."

If he had been told, at the time when he wrote these words, that a period would arrive when some—like me, for instance—would regret even that time, the poor Marquis d'Argenson would have doubtless been very much astonished. Therefore, what do I do ? Why, I live much with the past, a little with the exiles. I try to revive extinct society, to recall the memories of forgotten men, those who were scented with ambergris instead of smelling of cigars—those who fought with their swords instead of their fists.

This, my dear friend, is why you are surprised when I talk, to hear me speak a language no longer used. This is why you say I am an amusing tale-teller. This is why my voice, the echo of the past, is so attentively listened to in even this degenerate age, which listens so little and so badly.

It is because at the close of the account, like the Venetians of the eighteenth century, who were forbidden by the sumptuary laws to wear anything but cloth and serge, we always love to see silk and velvet, and the beautiful brocades of gold with which the robes of our fore-fathers were decorated, unrolled before our eyes, even though we may no longer wear them.

Yours sincerely,
ALEXANDRE DUMAS.

CHAPTER I.

THE RUE DE DIANE AT FONTENAY-AUX-ROSES.

ON the first of September, in the year 1831, I received an invitation from one of my oldest friends, who held the office of chancellor of the private domains of the king, to commence the shooting season with his son, on his estate at Fontenay-aux-Roses. I was passionately fond of field sports at that period, and consequently as with most of a first-rate sportsmen, it was always a matter of grave deliberation as to where I should commence the season every year.

I frequently went to a farmer's, or oftener to a friend of my brother-in-law's, on whose lands I made my *début* in the noble science of Nimrod and Elzéar Blaze, by shooting my first hare. His farm lay between the forests of Compiègne and Villers-Cotterets, half a league from the pretty village of Morienval, and about a league from the magnificent ruins of Pierrefonds.

The two or three thousand acres of land which formed his estate presented a vast plain, almost surrounded by woods, and divided in the centre by a beautiful valley, scattered over which were numbers of little white houses situated among the green meadows and half hidden in the masses of autumnal-tinted trees ; indeed, some of them were so concealed amid the foliage that their existence would scarcely have been suspected but for the columns of bluish grey smoke, which rose vertically upwards ; protected at first by the shelter afforded by the adjacent mountains, but which, on reaching the upper currents of air, spread out like the tops of palm-trees in the direction of the wind.

It was in the plain and upon the sides of this valley that the game from the two forests met, as it were, upon neutral ground.

Upon the estate of Brassoire, therefore, we found game in abundance ; there was the buck and the pheasant in the woods, the hare upon the table-land, the rabbit on the slopes, and partridges in great numbers round the farm. M. Mocquet, for such was the name of our friend, was generally sure of our arrival ; we were out the whole of the day and the next morning, at two o'clock ; we returned to Paris, having bagged, between four or five of us, about a hundred and fifty head of game, of which we could never induce our host to accept a single one.

But in the year which I have mentioned, faithless to M. Mocquet, I yielded to the oft-repeated invitation of my old friend, the chancellor ; tempted by a picture sent me by his son—a distinguished pupil of the Roman school —which represented a view of the plain of Fontenay-aux-Roses, with stubble-fields full of hares, and lucerne-fields swarming with par-tridges.

I had never been to Fontenay-aux-Roses : no one knew less of the environs of Paris than I did. Whenever I rode beyond the barriers, it was almost invariably on a journey of five or six hundred leagues. All these things combined, therefore, induced me to accept my friend's invitation to change my destination that season.

At six o'clock in the evening I left Paris for Fontenay, with my head, as usual, projecting from the carriage window ; I crossed the Barrier d'Enfer, leaving the Rue de la Tombe-Issoire on my left and took the road to Orleans.

Issoire, as you are aware, is the name of a famous brigand, who, some centuries since, levied contributions on all travellers going to Lutèce. He was hung, at least I believe so, and interred on the spot which now bears his name, not far from the entrance to the catacombs.

The plain, which extends to Petit-Montrouge, presents a very singular aspect. In the midst of the artificially-raised meadow, carrot-fields, and plantations of beet-root, rise several square-looking forts, built of white stone, each of which has a toothed wheel attached to it, re-sembling a skeleton frame for illumination. Round the exterior circumference of the wheels are placed a number of wooden cross-bars, upon which the workman places first one foot and then the other alternately. This squirrel-like occupation, which gives the workman the ap-pearance of much motion although he never even changes his position, winds a rope round the nave of the wheel ; as it rises, this rope draws up a stone, dug from the bottom of the quarry

"Pale and haggard, his hair standing on end," &c.—Page 6.

and which, by this proceeding, gradually ascends to the surface of the earth.

As soon as the stone reaches the orifice, it is carried off by means of rollers to its appointed destination. Then the rope again descends into the depths of the earth to be hooked on to another burden, giving the modern Ixion a moment's repose : a cry from below, soon, however, announces that another stone is awaiting his efforts to raise it from its native bed, and then the same labour commences over again, only to commence and re-commence perpetually.

When his day's work is finished, the man has gone six leagues without changing his place : if he could really mount a step in height every time he plants his foot upon one of the spokes, at the end of twenty-three years he would arrive at the moon.

It is in the evening especially—that is to say at the hour when I traversed the plain which separates little Montrouge from the larger place of that name—that the landscape, owing to the immense number of wheels which whirl round in the declining light, assumes the most peculiar appearance. It resembles one of those engravings by Goya where the teeth-drawers are hunting the hanged men in a kind of dim obscurity.

About seven o'clock the wheels stop; the day's work is over.

This soft stone, which lies in blocks about fifty or sixty feet long and six or eight feet high, is the future Paris which is thus drawn from the bowels of the earth. The quarries from which it is dug, become larger and larger every day : they are the catacombs from which old Paris has arisen. This stone will form the

"Why should I go when I confess all,—when I tell you that I have killed her."—*Page* 8.

faubourgs of the enormous city, which gains imperceptibly on the country and enlarges its circumference day by day. In walking over the fields of Montrouge one is walking over interminable caverns. From time to time you observe a sinking of the soil, a sort of valley in miniature, a ripple on the bosom of the earth. This is where the upper stratum of gypsum, ill-supported from below, has given way or cracked, by which means a fissure is opened through which the water penetrates into the pit; the water drags down the earth with it, and from thence the sinking of the land: this is called a *fondis*.

If you were not aware of this, if you were ignorant that the beautiful soft-looking couch of green velvet which invites you to repose upon it rests upon air, you might chance to place your foot in one of these chinks and disappear like they did at Montanvert, between two walls of ice.

The inhabitants of these subterranean galleries have, as it were, a character, an existence, a physiognomy peculiar to themselves. Living in profound darkness, they acquire habits and instincts resembling those of animals of the night: they are silent and ferocious. We frequently hear of accidents occurring there; a prop is missing, a rope is broken, a man is crushed to death. On the surface of the earth we believe it was a misfortune; thirty feet below it is known to have been a crime.

The expression of the stone-cutter's countenance is generally sinister. In the daylight his eyes blink, and his voice, in the open air, is low and deep. Their hair, which is thick and shaggy, hangs down over their eyebrows, their beards make acquaintance only on Sundays with the razor : they wear a waistcoat which allows their sleeves of coarse grey linen to be visible, a leather apron, whitened by its contact with the stone, and blue linen trowsers. On one of their shoulders is worn a jacket folded in two, upon which rests the handle of the pickaxe, or mattock, with which, six days out of the seven, they dig the stone.

If there is a disturbance in the neighbourhood, it is generally found to be occasioned by some of the men whom we have been attempting to describe. When it is announced at the barrier d'Enfer:—"The stonecutters of Montrouge are coming," the inhabitants of the adjoining streets shake their heads and close their doors.

This, then, is the sight which presented itself to my view during the twilight hour, which, in the month of September, divides the night from the day; then it became dark, too dark to see, and I threw myself back in the carriage, where assuredly none of my companions had seen what I had seen. It is the same always—some men look at everything and see nothing.

We arrived at Fontenay about half past eight o'clock ; an excellent supper was provided for us, and after the supper we had a promenade in the garden.

Sorrento is a forest of orange-trees ; Fontenay is a bouquet of roses. Every house has its rose-tree which covers the whole of the wall, protected at the bottom by a small row of plants ; the surrounding air is laden with perfume, and when there is a strong breeze, it rains rose-leaves like it used to do at the Fête-Dieu, when we had such a fête.

At the lower extremity of the garden, we were told we should have had a magnificent view, had it been day. The lights alone, which were sprinkled here and there in the distance, indicated where lay the villages of Sceaux, Bagneux, De Chatillon, and Montrouge ; on the verge of the horizon, a long reddish-coloured line might be seen, from which a low, deep sound emanated like the breathing of a Leviathan—it was the respiration of Paris. They were obliged to send us to bed by force, as if we had been children. Beneath that superb sky, embroidered all over with golden stars, inhaling the perfumed breeze which swept by, we would willingly have awaited the day-break.

At five o'clock the next morning, we started on our shooting expedition, under the guidance of our host's son, who promised us mountains and marvels, and who, it is necessary to add, continued to boast about the quantity of game on the estate with the pertinacity worthy of a better cause.

By noon we had seen one rabbit and four partridges ; the rabbit was fired at and missed by my companion on the right, one partridge was missed by my companion on the left, and two out of the remaining three fell to me.

At Brassoire I should have sent three or four hares and eight or ten brace of partridges to the farm long before noon.

I am fond of the sport, but I hate promenades, especially promenades through stubble fields ; so, under pretence of exploring a tract of lucerne which lay far away to the left, and in which I was pretty sure of finding nothing, I broke the line and made my escape.

But that which I did see in the above-mentioned field, that which had inspired me with a wish to retreat thither for more than two hours, but which I had hitherto been prevented from doing, was a deeply cut road, which, by concealing me from the eyes of the other sportsmen, would allow of my return through Sceaux to Fontenay-aux-Roses.

I was not mistaken ; as the hour of one sounded from the parish clock, I reached the outskirts of the village.

I followed for some distance the course of a wall which appeared to enclose a very charming residence ; just as I arrived where the Rue de Diane crosses the Grande Rue, I perceived a man running towards me, on the same side as the church, and of such an extraordinary aspect, that I stopped and cocked both the barrels of my gun, actuated by a natural instinct of self-preservation.

But pale and haggard, his hair standing on end, his eyes starting from their sockets, his clothes in wild disorder and his hands red with blood, the man passed close by me without even perceiving me. His eye was both fixed and glaring at the same time. He seemed carried along with the uncontrollable velocity of a body rolling down a mountain, and yet his agitated, choking respiration, appeared to proceed more from terror than from fatigue.

Where the two roads met he left the Grande Rue and rushed into the Rue de Diane into which the house opened whose garden wall I had been following for the last seven or eight minutes. My eyes alighted at the same instant upon the door which was painted green, and surmounted by the figure 2. The man stretched out his hand to pull the bell long before he could by any possibility reach it ; at length he did so, and pulled it violently ; then immediately sank down in a sitting posture on one of the spur-stones which served as out-posts to the doorway, where he remained, perfectly motionless, with his arms hanging down by his sides and his head sunk upon his breast.

I turned down the street, for I felt certain that this man had been a principal actor in some terrible and mysterious drama.

Behind him, on either side of the street, several persons upon whom he had doubtless produced the same impression as he had upon me, came out of their houses and stood gazing at him, evidently as much astonished at his appearance as I was myself.

In answer to the violent summons which he had given by the bell, a small door, close to the larger one, was opened and an old woman, eighty or eighty-five years of age, appeared at it. "Ah! is that you, Jacquemin," she exclaimed," what is the matter ?"

"Is the mayor at home ?" asked the person thus addressed, in a low, husky voice.

"Yes."

"Well then, mother Antoine, go and tell him that I have murdered my wife and am come to give myself up to justice."

The old woman uttered a loud cry, which was responded to by several exclamations of surprise and horror from those who were standing round and were near enough to hear this terrible avowal.

I myself involuntarily made a step backwards, where encountering the trunk of a lime tree I leant myself against it.

All the other spectators who were within ear-shot, however, remained motionless.

As for the murderer, he had slipped down from the spur-stone to the ground, as if, after having pronounced the fatal words, every particle of strength had deserted him.

Mother Antoine disappeared, leaving the little door wide open. She was evidently gone to deliver Jacquemin's message to her master.

Five minutes afterwards, the person whom he had desired to see, appeared upon the threshold of the door.

He was accompanied by two other men.

I again glanced at the picture which the street presented to me.

Jacquemin had fallen down, and was almost lying on the ground, as I have already described. The mayor of Fontenay-aux-Roses, whom mother Antoine had been to seek, stood over him, looking down upon him from his full height, for he was a tall man. In the doorway, pressing eagerly forward, stood the two men who had accompanied the mayor, and of whom we shall have to speak more particularly hereafter. I was leaning against the trunk of a lime-tree which stood in the Grande Rue, from whence I could distinctly see all that was passing in the Rue de Diane. On my left was a group, composed of a man, a woman, and a child; the child was crying for its mother to take it up in her arms. Behind this group a baker was looking out from a window in the upper story, and talking to his boy down below, asking him if it was not Jacquemin the stone-cutter who had just rushed by; and farther on, stood a farrier at the threshold of his door, thrown in front into deep shade but lighted up behind by the strong glare of his forge at which an apprentice continued to blow the bellows.

So much for the Grande Rue.

As for the Rue de Diane, apart from the principal group which we have already described, it was entirely deserted, except at the farther extremity, where two gendarmes were just making their appearance: they were returning after having made the round of the plain in order to examine the licences for carrying arms, and perfectly unsuspicious of the work in store for them, were riding slowly towards us.

The clock chimed a quarter past one.

CHAPTER II.

SERGEANT'S ALLEY.

With the last vibration of the bell was mingled the sound of the mayor's voice as he addressed himself to the man, saying: "Jacquemin, I hope mother Antoine is beside herself; she has just come to me, and she says you sent her, to tell me that your wife is dead, and that it is you who have killed her!"

"It is the real truth, monsieur," replied Jacquemin. "You had better have me taken to prison at once, and guillotine me as soon as possible."

So saying, he attempted to rise, by helping himself up by the spur-stone with his elbow, but finding all his efforts fruitless, he fell back again as if the bones of his legs were broken.

"Come, come," said the mayor, "you must be mad."

"Look at my hands," he replied.

And he held up two bloody hands to which the shrivelled fingers gave the appearance of claws.

And truly the left hand was red up to the wrist, the right one up to the elbow. Besides this, a stream of fresh blood was creeping down the thumb of the right hand, proving that the victim, in its mortal struggle, had, in all probability, bitten the assassin's hand.

During this conversation the two gendarmes had approached close to us, and halted about ten paces from the principal actors in this scene, at which they sat looking gravely down from their saddles.

The mayor beckoned to them; they dismounted, throwing their horses' bridles to a boy wearing a policeman's cap, who appeared to belong to the force.

They then approached Jacquemin, and lifted him up by taking hold of him under the arm-pits.

He let them do so without making the least resistance, with the utter abandonment of a man whose whole soul is absorbed in one idea.

At that instant the commissary of police and the doctor arrived, having been informed of what was passing.

"Ah! come here, Monsieur Robert. I am glad to see you, Monsieur Cousin," cried the mayor.

M. Robert was the doctor; M. Cousin, the commissary of police.

"I am glad you are come, for I was just on the point of sending for you."

"Well! here we are, what is the matter?" asked the doctor in the merriest tone in the world; "a little affair of murder, is it not?"

Jacquemin did not utter a word in reply.

"Come, come, Master Jacquemin," continued the doctor, "tell us, is it true that you have killed your wife?"

Jacquemin did not breathe a syllable.

"At all events," said the mayor, "he has come here to accuse himself of the deed in question; but I am in hopes he is labouring under some temporary hallucination, and is not really guilty of such a dreadful crime."

"Jacquemin," said the commissary of police, "why do you not answer? Have you really killed your wife?"

The same silence.

"In that case, we must go and see for ourselves," said the doctor, addressing himself to the mayor: "is not his residence in Sergeant's Alley."

"Yes," replied the two gendarmes.

"Well, M. Ledru," said the doctor, addressing himself to the mayor, "let us proceed at once to Sergeant's Alley."

"I will not go there! I will not go there!" cried Jacquemin, tearing himself away from the

"She was on her knees like a guilty one—like one condemned. I raised the sword."—*Page* 14.

two gendarmes with such a sudden and un-expected movement that had he attempted to escape, certes he might have been a hundred paces off before any one would have recovered sufficiently from their surprise to have pursued him.

"Why do you object to go there?" asked the mayor.

"Why should I go, when I confess all, when I tell you that I have killed her; that I killed her with the great two-handed sword which I took from the Artillery Museum, last year. Take me to prison; I have nothing more to do with this world: take me to prison!"

The doctor and M. Ledru exchanged glances.

"My friend," said the commissary of police, who, like M. Ledru, believed that Jacquemin was labouring under some temporary derange-ment of intellect, "my friend, it is absolutely necessary that you should go there to guide justice in the right track."

"In what does justice require to be guided?" said Jacquemin; "you will find the body in the cellar, and near the body, you will find the head on a sack of plaster; as for me, take me away to prison."

"Indeed you must come with us," said the commissary of police.

"Oh! my God! my God!" cried Jacquemin, with an expression of terror perfectly appalling. "Oh! my God! my God! if I had known this."

"Well, what would you have done?" asked the commissary of police.

"I would have killed myself!"

M. Ledru shook his head, and glancing at the commissary of police, seemed to say, "There is

"And, stooping down, he picked up a sword with an enormous blade."—*Page* 11.

something more under all this. Come, my friend," he continued, addressing himself to the murderer, "explain all this to me, tell me alone."

"Yes, yes; I will tell you, you shall know all, M. Ledru, ask on, ask me what you will."

"How is it, since you were bold enough to commit the murder, that you have not sufficient courage to enable you to face your victim? Has anything occurred beyond what you have told us, something which you do not like to tell us?"

"Oh, yes! something very terrible."

"Well! what is it? go on."

"Oh, no! you would say it was not true; you would say that I was mad."

"Never mind; what has occurred, tell me?"

"I will tell you, but you only."

He approached M. Ledru.

The gendarmes attempted to hold him back; the mayor made a sign to them, and they immediately let the prisoner go.

Besides, had he even wished to escape, it would now have been impossible, for half the population of Fontenay-aux-Roses were crowding together in the Grande Rue and the Rue de Diane. Jacquemin, as I said before, approached close to M. Ledru's ear, and said in a low voice—

"M. Ledru, do you believe that a head could speak after it was separated from the body?"

M. Ledru started and uttered a cry of surprise; he turned visibly pale.

"Do you believe it could? say if you do?" asked Jacquemin.

M. Ledru made a great effort: "Yes," he said, "I believe it might."

"Well!—well!—it spoke!"

"What?"

"The head—Jeanne's head."

"Are you sure?"

"Yes; I say that her eyes were wide open, she moved her lips; she looked hard at me. I say that when she looked at me, she opened her mouth and said, "Wretch!" As he uttered these words, which he had intended that M. Ledru alone should hear, but which, nevertheless, could be heard by all around him, Jacquemin looked perfectly hideous.

"Oh! that is a fine idea," cried the doctor, laughing; "she spoke, did she?—spoke after her head was cut off? Famous! famous!!"

Jacquemin turned sharply round: "When did I tell you that?" he said.

"Come, come!" said the commissary of police, "this makes it all the more necessary that we should proceed at once to the place where the crime was committed. Gendarmes! conduct the prisoner thither."

Jacquemin cried out and tried to get away from them. "No, no!" he shrieked, "you may cut me in pieces if you like, but I will not go there."

"Come, my friend," said M. Ledru, "if it is true that you have committed the terrible crime of which you accuse yourself, this will be a kind of expiation. Besides," he added in a lower tone, "resistance is useless; if you will not go there of yourself, they will carry you there by force."

"Well, then," said Jacquemin, "if it must be so, I will go on one condition; if you will promise me one thing, M. Ledru?"

"What is it?"

"That you will not leave me for a moment while we are in the cellar."

"Very well."

"You will let me hold you by the hand?"

"Yes."

"I will go then," he said.

And drawing from his pocket a checked handkerchief, he wiped away the large drops of moisture from his forehead.

We directed our steps towards Sergent's Alley.

The commissary of police and the doctor went first; Jacquemin and the two gendarmes followed.

Behind them walked M. Ledru and the two friends who had stood at his door with him. Then followed the crowd, rolling along like a surging, swelling billow, with which I was myself carried along.

It was not long before we entered Sergeant's Alley. It was a narrow lane situated on the left side of the high street, and sloped down to a large, dilapidated, wooden gate, opening by two large wings, in one of which was cut out a small door.

This little door hung only by one hinge.

All, at the first view, looked perfectly calm and tranquil; a rose-tree flourished at the gate, and near the rose-tree, upon a stone bench, lay a large cat basking in the warm twilight. As soon as she saw the large crowd approaching, and heard the noise, she became alarmed, and disappeared through the cellar grating.

When we had reached the gate which I have described, Jacquemin stopped.

The gendarmes attempted to force him through it.

"M. Ledru," said he, turning round, "M. Ledru, you promised not to leave me."

"Very well! here I am," replied the mayor.

"Give me your arm, let me hold your arm."

And he staggered as if he was about to fall.

M. Ledru approached him, made a sign to the gendarmes to let go of him, and gave him his arm. "I will answer for him," he said.

From that moment it was evident that M. Ledru was no longer the mayor of a commune, investigating the particulars of a suspected crime, but a philosopher exploring the mysterious regions of the unknown.

The singular part of his research, however, was that his guide was an assassin.

The doctor and the commissary of police entered the gates first, then M. Ledru and Jacquemin, then the two gendarmes, and then a few privileged persons, in which class I was fortunately included, thanks to my acquaintance with the gendarmes, to whom I was no longer a stranger, having had the honour to meet them that morning in the plains, where I had showed them my licence for bearing arms.

The door was closed on the remainder of the population, who accordingly remained grumbling outside.

A small house stood in the yard, and towards this house we directed our steps.

Within, nothing indicated the terrible event which had occurred; everything appeared to be in its place: the bed, with its green serge curtains stood in the alcove; at the head of the bed hung a black wooden crucifix surmounted by a branch of consecrated boxwood, somewhat withered since Easter; upon the chimney-piece was an image of the infant Jesus, in wax, lying among some flowers, between two chandeliers of the style of Louis XVI. which had once been plated with silver; and on the wall hung four coloured engravings in black wooden frames, representing the four quarters of the globe.

A cloth was spread on the table, and on the hearth stood a pot which appeared to be boiling, near these was a cuckoo clock, which sung out the half-hours.

"Well," said the doctor, in his jovial sort of tone; "I see nothing yet.".

"Go through the door on the right," murmured Jacquemin in a hollow voice.

They followed the direction which the prisoner indicated and we found ourselves in a narrow passage, in one corner of which a trap-door stood open, through which a light trembled, which evidently proceeded from somewhere below.

"There! there!" cried Jacquemin, clinging to M. Ledru's arm with one hand while with the other he pointed to the entrance to the cellar.

"Ah! ah!" said the doctor, in a low tone, to the commissary of police, with the habitual kind of laugh those persons indulge in on whom nothing makes an impression, merely because they believe in nothing:—"it would seem that Madame Jacquemin followed the precept of Master Adam;" and he sang:—

"If I die let me be buried
In a cellar wherein is * * *"

"Silence!" interrupted Jacquemin, whose face was perfectly livid, while his hair stood on end, and the perspiration streamed down in large drops from his forehead:—"do not sing here!"

Struck by the tone of the man's voice, the doctor immediately ceased.

He then began to descend the steps into the cellar, but stopping almost directly, exclaimed "What is this?"

And stooping down, he picked up a sword with an enormous blade.

This was the two-handled sword which Jacquemin had confessed he had taken from the artillery museum on the 29th of July, 1830: the weapon was covered with blood.

The commissary of police took it out of the doctor's hands.

"Do you recognise the sword?" he said, turning to Jacquemin.

"Yes," was the reply. "Go on! go on! let us finish all this?"

This weapon was the first landmark of the murder which had yet been discovered.

They then descended into the cellar, all keeping the same rank as before.

The doctor and the commissary of police went first, then M. Ledru and Jacquemin, then the mayor's two friends, then the gendarmes, and finally the few privileged persons in whose number I was included.

As I reached the seventh step, my eye was enabled to pierce the obscurity, and embrace the whole of the terrible picture which I will now attempt to describe.

The first object which arrested the attention, was a headless corpse, lying near a cask, the top of which was partly turned and allowed a small stream of wine to escape, which, as it flowed down formed itself into a little pool, and finally soaked away beneath the flags.

The body of the murdered woman lay in a somewhat distorted position, as though, while turning over, it had been taken in the death-struggle, a movement which the legs were unable to follow.

The dress on one side was turned back as high as the knee.

It was evident that the death-blow had been dealt while the unfortunate victim was on her knees before the cask, filling a bottle which had afterwards fallen from her hands, and was now lying at her side.

The upper portion of the body was swimming in a perfect sea of blood.

Upon a sack of plaster which was standing against the wall, resembling a bust upon a column, we perceived or rather we suspected there stood a head, for it was almost entirely concealed by the long light hair which fell over it; a dark stream of blood stained the sack from the top half-way down.

The doctor and commissary of police had already gone round the corpse and were now standing opposite the staircase.

M. Ledru's two friends also went down into the cellar accompanied by two or three of the more inquisitive ones, who were anxious to examine all the details.

At the foot of the stairs stood Jacquemin, who could not be persuaded to go farther than the bottom step. The two gendarmes stood behind him.

Farther back were five or six persons with myself among them; we formed a group about half way up the staircase.

The whole of this interior was but dimly lighted by the flickering glare of a small candle which stood on the cask from which the wine was slowly running, and opposite which, lay the corpse of Jacquemin's wife.

"Bring a table and a chair," said the commissary of police, "and let us proceed at once to draw up the report."

CHAPTER III.

THE OFFICIAL REPORT.

THE articles which I have mentioned, were handed to the commissary of police. He fixed the table in a convenient position, seated himself at it, asked for the candle, which the doctor passed over to him by stepping over the corpse as he did so, took an inkstand and pens and paper from his pocket, and commenced drawing up the report.

While he was writing the preamble, the doctor made a step towards the head, which stood on the sack of plaster, for the purpose of examining it, but the commissary stopped him.

"Do not touch anything," he said; "regularity before everything."

"Very true," said the doctor resuming his former position. There were several moments' silence, during which not a sound was heard except the scratching of the commissary's pen on the rough government paper, where the lines might be seen succeeding each other with a rapidity which proved that the writer was well accustomed to such formulas.

When he had written several lines, he paused and looked around him.

"Who are willing to serve as witnesses?" he asked, addressing himself to the mayor.

"These two gentlemen, first of all," said M. Ledru, pointing to his two friends who were standing close to the commissary, and formed the background to the picture.

"Very well."

He then turned to me.

"And this gentleman also, provided he has no objection to seeing his name in the official report."

"None in the least," I replied.

"Come down here, if you please," said the commissary of police.

I felt some repugnance at the idea of approaching the corpse. From where I stood, several minor details, without altogether escaping my notice, appeared to me less hideous, lost in the half-obscurity which threw an almost poetic veil over their horrors, than if I had examined them more closely.

"Is it absolutely necessary?" I asked.

"What?"

"That I should come down."

"Oh! no. Remain there if you prefer it."

The cellar—the scene of the murder.—*Page* 11.

I gave an inclination of the head, as much as to say—I would rather remain where I am. The commissary of police then turned towards M. Ledru's two friends, and addressing the one who stood nearest to him said, with a volubility of a man accustomed to ask such questions, "Give me your name, surname, age, rank or profession, and place of residence?"—"My name is Jean Louis-Alliette," replied the person to whom he spoke; called Ettéilla by way of anagram; "I am of the literary profession, and live at No. 20, Rue de l'Ancienne Comédie."

"You have forgotten your age," said the commissary of police.

"Am I to give my real age, or the age I am generally supposed to be?"

"Tell me your real age; *parbleu!* no one has two ages."

"Begging your pardon, Monsieur, there are several persons, such as Cagliostro, the Count of St. Germains, and the Wandering Jew, for example"—

"Do you mean to say that you are either Cagliostro, the Count of St. Germains, or the Wandering Jew?" asked the commissary, frowning heavily, evidently under the idea that he was being trifled with.

"No, but"—

"He is seventy-five," said M. Ledru; "put down seventy-five years of age, Monsieur Cousin."

"Very well," said the commissary of police. And he accordingly put it down.

"And you, sir?" he continued, addressing himself to M. Ledru's other friend, and repeating precisely the same questions as before.

The official report.—*Page* 11.

"My name is Pierre-Joseph Moulle, I am sixty-one years of age, priest, attached to the Church of St. Sulpice, and live at No. 11, Rue Servandoni," replied the gentleman whom he addressed, in a soft, low voice.

"And you, sir," he continued turning to me.

"Alexandre Dumas, dramatic author, twenty-seven years of age, living in Paris, at No. 21, Rue de l'Université," I replied.

At this M. Ledru turned round and made me a low bow, which I returned with the best grace I could assume.

"Well!" said the commissary of police: "now let us see if it is all correct, gentlemen, and tell me if you have any observations to make.

So saying, in the monotonous, nasal tone, which usually appertains to public functionaries, he read as follows:

"To-day, being the first of September, 1831, at the second hour of the relieve guard, having been informed that a murder had been committed in the town of Fontenay-aux-Roses, upon the person of Marie-Jeanne Ducoudray, by the under-mentioned Pierre Jacquemin, her husband, and having further heard that the murderer was at the house occupied by Jean-Pierre Ledru, mayor of the said town of Fontenay-aux-Roses, where he had of his own free will, confessed that he was author of the said crime, I hastened in my own proper person to the house inhabited by the afore-named Jean-Pierre Ledru at No. 2, Rue de Diane; on arriving at which domicile, accompanied by M. Sebastian Robert, Doctor of Medicine, a resident of the said town of Fontenay-aux-Roses, and finding that the above-named Pierre Jacquemin was already in the hands of the police, we made him repeat before us that he was the author of the said murder upon the person of his wife ; upon which we summoned him to follow us to the house where the said murder had been committed. At first he refused to do so ; but at length he yielded to the persuasions of M. Ledru, the mayor ; upon which we proceeded at once to Sergeant's Alley, where the house occupied by Pierre Jacquemin is situated. On our arrival at this house (where we closed the outer gates to prevent the crowd which followed us from overcrowding it), we entered the ordinary chamber used by the family, in which there were no indications of the crime that had been committed ; then, at the instigation of the said Jacquemin himself, we passed from the first chamber into a second, in the corner of which was a trap-door then standing wide open, and giving access to a flight of steps. These steps having been pointed out to us as leading down to a cellar where we should discover the body of the murdered woman, we descended the steps, upon one of which the doctor found a sword, with a cross handled hilt and a broad sharp blade, which sword the said Jacquemin confessed to have taken from the Artillery Museum during the Revolution of July, and to have committed the above-mentioned crime with it. Farther, on the floor of the cellar, we found the body of the woman Jacquemin lying turned over on its back and swimming in a sea of blood, having the head separated from the trunk. The said head was placed upright upon a sack of plaster leaning against the wall, and the said Jacquemin did recognize the aforesaid corpse and this head as being those of his wife, in the presence of M. Jean-Pierre Ledru, mayor of the town of Fontenay-aux-Roses ; M. Sebastian Robert, Doctor of Medicine, residing in the aforesaid town of Fontenay-aux-Roses ; M. Jean-Louis Alliette, commonly called Ettéilla, of the literary profession, aged seventy-five, living in Paris, at No. 20, Rue de l'Ancienne Comédie ; M. Pierre-Joseph Moulle, aged sixty-one, a priest attached to the Church of St. Sulpice, living in Paris, at No. 11, Rue Servandoni ; and of M. Alexandre Dumas, dramatic author, twenty-seven years of age, living in Paris, at No. 21, Rue de l'Université : we therefore proceeded to examine the accused as follows :—

"Is this correct, gentlemen ?" asked the commissary of police, turning towards us with an air of evident satisfaction.

"Perfectly so, monsieur !" we replied unanimously.

"Very well ! We will now therefore examine the accused."

Then turning towards the prisoner, who during the whole of this preamble, had remained standing and breathing hard like a person oppressed by some terrible weight : "Prisoner," he said, "give me your name, surname, age, place of residence, and occupation."

"Will this last much longer ?" asked the prisoner, in a tone of perfect misery and despair.

"Reply to my questions : what is your name ?"

"Pierre Jacquemin ?"

"Your age ?"

"Forty-one."

"Where do you live ?"

"You know that, for you are in my house at this moment."

"Never mind : the law requires that you should answer this question yourself."

"In Sergeant's Alley, then."

"What is your occupation ?"

"I am a stone-cutter."

"You confess that you are guilty of this crime ?"

"Yes."

"Tell us the cause which led you to commit it, and the circumstances under which it was committed."

"The cause which led me to commit it ?" said Jacquemin, "ah! that is unnecessary : that must remain a secret for ever between me and she who lies there."

"Still there can be no effect without a cause."

"The cause I tell you, you shall not know. As for the circumstances, as you call them, am I to tell you them ?"

"Yes."

"Well, I will do so. When people work under the earth like we work, in solitude and darkness, if anything happens to put one out, you see, we hate our own souls and terrible ideas come into our heads."

"Oh! oh!" interrupted the commissary of police, "you acknowledge that this crime was premeditated then ?"

"Have I not told you already that I acknowledge everything ? is not that enough ?"

"Very well, go on."

"So this terrible idea came and came again ; it was to kill Jeanne. It troubled me for more than a month ; the heart prevented the head ; at last one of my companions said a word to me ;—that decided me."

"What was that word ?"

"Oh! no, that is one of the things which it does not signify about your knowing. Well, this morning, I said 'Jeanne, I am not going to my work to-day : I shall enjoy myself just as if it was a holiday : I shall go and play bowls with some of my companions. Take care that dinner is ready exactly at one o'clock, do you hear.' 'Yes ; but—' 'Come, come, no observations ; dinner at one o'clock, remember.' 'Very well,' said Jeanne ; and she went out to look for the large pot. While she was gone out, instead of going to the bowling-green, I took the sword which you have there ; I had already sharpened it on a grindstone. I went down into the cellar, and hid myself behind the casks, saying, she will be sure to come down into the cellar to draw the wine and then—we shall see. How long I lay there crouched down behind the casks, for there is little space enough there, I can't tell you—I do not know : I was in a fever of mind and body : my heart beat fast, and everything around looked red, like it does in the night. And then a voice came and kept whispering in my ear and all around me, and kept repeating the words which my companion said to me yesterday.

"But will you not tell us that word ?" persisted the commissary.

"No, no, it is useless to ask me ; I have already told you that you shall never know it. At last I heard the rustling of a gown, and then a step coming. I perceived a light, too, trembling in the distance. Then I saw a foot descending the first step, then the other, then the whole body, and then the head; I saw the head so plain—she held a candle in her hand. Ah! I said, that is right, and then I repeated in a low voice the word which my companion had said to me. All this time she kept approaching nearer and nearer. On my soul one would have thought she had some presentiment that evil was about to happen to her. She seemed frightened and glanced round on every side; but I was well concealed and did not even breathe; then she knelt down in front of the cask, put the bottle under the tap and turned the peg. Then I got up. You understand, she was keeling down. The noise which the wine made as it ran into the bottle I knew would prevent her from hearing me. However, I approached her without making the least noise; she was kneeling down just like a guilty person would kneel, just as if she had been condemned. I raised the sword—and—ha! I do not know whether she cried out or not; her head rolled down. At that time I did not wish to die—I wanted to save myself—I thought I would dig a hole in the cellar and bury her there. I tried to seize the head but it rolled away from me, while the body also started aside. I had brought a sack of plaster all ready to hide the blood: I caught hold of the head, or rather, the head caught hold of me. See here!"

"What! the head caught hold of you?" exclaimed the doctor. "What the deuce do you mean by that?"

"I tell you it bit hold of me as hard as it could, and here are the marks of the teeth."

So saying, he held up his right hand where a large bite had wounded the thumb.

"I tell you," he continued, "she would not leave go of me. I put the head upon the sack of plaster; I held it hard against the wall with my left hand and tried with all my might to tear away my other hand; but after an instant the teeth unclosed of themselves. I took away my hand: and then—but perhaps it is only my fancy, you see, I thought that the head was still alive, the eyes were wide open and stared full at me, I saw them plain, for the candle was standing on the cask, and then the lips—the lips—moved, and as they opened, said :—'Wretch, I was innocent!'"

I do not know what effect this confession had upon the others; but for my own part, I know that the perspiration streamed down from my forehead.

"Ah! this is too much!" cried the doctor, "the eyes looked at you, and the lips spoke."

"Listen, sir; you are a doctor, and you believe in nothing that is natural; but I swear that the head which you see there—there, do you understand? I swear that that head bit hold of me: I swear that that head said to me: 'Wretch, I was innocent!' And to prove that she did say it to me, well! I wished to save myself after I had killed her? Jeanne, is it not so? but instead of saving myself did I not run to M. Ledru's house, to give myself up as her murderer? Is this true or not? M. Ledru, answer me, pray."

"Yes, Jacquemin," replied the mayor, in a tone which proved that he believed it all.

"Examine the head, doctor," said the commissary of police.

"When I am gone, Monsieur Robert, when I am gone!" cried Jacquemin.

"What, stupid! are you still afraid it will speak to you?" said the doctor, taking up the light and going towards the sack of plaster.

"In the name of Heaven! M. Ledru," said Jacquemin, "let them take me away first. I beseech you to tell them to take me away!"

"Sir," said the mayor, making a gesture to stop the doctor,—"You have nothing further to ask this unfortunate man, allow me to have him conducted to prison. When the law orders that the accused should be confronted with his victim, it supposes that he has sufficient strength to support it."

"But the official report?" said the commissary.

"It is almost finished."

"It is necessary that the accused should sign it."

"He can sign it in prison."

"Yes! yes!" cried Jacquemin, "I will sign everything you like in the prison."

"Very well, be it so," said the commissary,

"Gendarmes! conduct this man to prison," said M. Ledru.

"Oh! thank you, M. Ledru, thank you," said Jacquemin, with an expression of the most profound gratitude.

And taking the two gendarmes by the arms he dragged them up the steps with almost incredible force.

With the man, disappeared in my eyes all the interest of the drama.

There remained nothing in the cellar but two hideous objects: a body without a head, and a head without a body.

I turned towards M. Ledru.

"Monsieur," I said, "may I be permitted to retire, of course holding myself ready at any time when I may be called upon to sign the official report.

"Certainly, sir; but on one condition however."

"What is that?"

"That you will come and sign the report in my house."

"With pleasure, monsieur; at what hour?"

"In about an hour's time, I will shew you over it; it formerly belonged to Scarron, and will interest you."

"In an hour's time, then, monsieur, I will be with you."

I bowed, and in my turn ascended the steps: when I reached the upper one, I turned to give a final glance at the cellar below.

The doctor, M. Robert, candle in hand, was putting back the hair from the forehead of the head: it was that of a young and beautiful woman, as far as one could judge, for the eyes were closed and the lips contracted and livid.

"That fool of a Jacquemin!" said the doctor, "to persist in it that a head could speak after it was cut off from the body; unless, indeed, he invented it all to make us believe he is mad: not badly played either—there were certainly some extenuating circumstances."

"The doctor, candle in hand, was pulling back the hair from the forehead."—*Page* 15.

CHAPTER IV.

THE HOUSE OF SCARRON.

An hour after the occurrence before mentioned, I was at the house of M. Ledru. I met him in the court.

"Ah!" said he, perceiving me, "you are there, and so much the better am I pleased, for I really should be glad of a little chat with you before I present you to your fellow guests of mine—for of course you dine with us?"

"But, really, you must excuse me"—

"I shall admit of no excuse: you have ran against me on a Tuesday, so much the worse for you. Tuesday, you must know, is my day: all my friends who encounter me on a Tuesday I seize as my own lawful property. After dinner, you shall be free to depart or to stay. Ordinarily I dine invariably at two o'clock, but to-day being an extraordinary affair, we shall dine at half-past three or four. I should say also, that the present gives me an opportunity, not only of presenting you to your fellow guests, but of giving you some information respecting each of them."

"Some information?"

"Yes—you see they are personages, like those in the *Barber of Seville* and of *Figaro*, requiring to have their presence preluded by a sort of explanatory argument, detailing their costumes and characters. We shall, however, begin with the house in which we are."

"You told me, if I don't mistake, sir, that it was once the property of Scarron."

"Yes, it was here that the future wife of King Louis the Fourteenth, whilst in waiting to amuse

The arrest of Solange by the revolutionary patrole.

the man who had survived the faculty of being amused, nursed the poor *cul-de-jalte*,* her first husband. You shall see her chamber."

"Madame de Maintenon's?"

"No: Madame Scarron's—don't confound the two—the chamber of Madame Maintenon is at Versailles or Saint Cyr. Come!"

We ascended the grand staircase, and found ourselves in a corridor overlooking the court.

"Hold," said M. Ledru to me, "look at the bust which you are touching, Mr. Poet: it is that of the pure-minded Phébus, who lived in 1650."

"Ah! ah! the Chart of Affection."

"The Voyage and Return, drawn by Scarron, and annotated by the hand of his wife—neither more nor less."

* A cripple who slides along on his back.—*Trans.*

In fact, the two charts were fixed between two of the windows. They were drawn by a pen, upon a large sheet of paper pasted on card-board.

"You see," continued M. Ledru, "that great blue serpent, that is the Flood of Tenderness; those little pigeon holes are the Cottages of Little Cares, Billets-doux, and Mystery. You see here the Hotel of Desire, the Valley of Sweets, the Bridge of Sighs, the Forest of Jealousy, all peopled with monsters like those of Armida. Lastly, in the middle of the Lake from whence the flood takes its rise, you may see the Palace of Perfect Contentment; that is the whole extent of the voyage: the termination of its course."

"The Devil! but what is this—a volcano?"

"Yes; and one that sometimes turns the whole

country topsyturvy. It is the Volcano of the Passions."

"This is not, surely, the Chart of Mademoiselle Scudery ?"

"No: it is the invention of Madame Paul Scarron. And that one—

"The other ?"

"The other—that is the Return. You see that the flood has overflowed its banks, its waters have been augmented by the tears of those who have traversed its course. Here you see the Hamlet of Ennui, the Hotel of Regret, the Island of Repentance. Is it not very ingenious ?"

"Would you have the kindness to permit me to copy it ?"

"Oh—whenever you please. Now, will you see Madame Scarron's chamber ?"

"Gladly."

"Here it is," said M. Ledru, as he opened a door, and made me pass before him into a chamber.

"Although this is now my property," said the mayor, "yet, with the exception of the books with which it is encumbered, I can assure you that it is in the same state as it was in the time of its illustrious proprietress; there is the identical alcove, the same bed, the veritable furniture: these toilet cabinets were her own."

"And the chamber of Scarron ?"

"Ah! Scarron's chamber was at the other end of the corridor; but as respects that, it is private; no one enters it, in fact, it is a secret chamber—Blue-Beard's cabinet.

"The deuce !"

"It is so, in truth. I have my own little mysteries, public functionary though I be. But come, I'll show you some other things."

M. Ledru led the way; we descended the grand staircase, and made our entry into the saloon. Like the rest of the house, this part of it had peculiar characteristics: the hangings were of paper, the primitive hues of which it would have been difficult to determine; along the walls were ranged a double rank of arm-chairs, flanked by another row of chairs, all covered with old tapestry; here and there, tables and lamp-stands for play: and, in the midst of all this, like a Leviathan among the fishes of the ocean, a gigantic bureau extending from the wall, on which it rested at one end, to about one-third of the saloon—a bureau covered entirely with books, pamphlets, and journals, in the midst of which towered above the rest, as a king over his courtiers, files of the *Constitutionel*, the favourite journal of M. Ledru.

The saloon was empty: my fellow-guests were all promenading in the garden, which, as we could see from every window in the saloon, extended along the whole front. M. Ledru went to his bureau, and opened an immense drawer on the right, in which were deposited numerous little packets, resembling those sold by gardeners and nurserymen. The objects which were contained in these packets were themselves enclosed in ticketed papers.

"See here," said he to me; "here is something for you to look at, historian as you are, which will interest you even more than the Chart of Tenderness. It is a collection of reliques,—not of saints—but of kings."

In fact, each paper enveloped a bone, or some hair, either from head or beard. Here were gathered together, a knee-pan of Charles IX.; a thumb of Francis I.; a piece of the cranium of Louis XIV.; a rib of Henry IV.; and hair of Louis XIII. Each monarch had furnished a sample of his own proper person; and amongst all these vestiges of royalty it would not have been difficult to have composed a skeleton which should have perfectly represented the entire French monarchy: of which, by the by, many of the principal members have been long missing.

There was also among this unique collection a tooth of Abelard, and one formerly belonging to Heloise,—two fine white incisors, which, when covered by their humid and trembling lips, had often perhaps encountered each other in a thrilling kiss.

But from whence came this collection of dry bones ?

M. Ledru had presided in his official capacity at the exhumation of the kings at St. Denis, and he had taken from each tomb, then broken into, a sample of its contents.

M. Ledru allowed me to pass some time in reviewing these vestiges of mortality, when, seeing that my curiosity was satisfied, and that I had gone through the whole of his ticketed papers, he said:

"Now then, we have occupied ourselves quite long enough with the dead, let us pass on to the living."

So saying, he led me to one of the windows, from any one of which, as I have said, the garden presented itself immediately underneath.

"You have a charming garden," said I to him.

"The curé's garden, with its quincunx of lime-trees, its collections of dahlias and roses, its bowers of trailing vines, and its espaliers of peach and apricot trees; you shall see all this: but for the present, let us occupy ourselves not with the garden, but rather with those who are now promenading in it."

"Well, then, tell me in the first place if that is not M. Alliette, better known by his anagram of *Etteila*, who asked if we wished to know his real age, or merely the age which he apparently was; he looks to me to have the appearance of a man about sixty-five, as you told him."

"Exactly," answered M. Ledru, "I shall commence the account with him. Have you read Hoffman ?"

"Yes—Why ?"

"Good: he is a follower of Hoffman. His life has been spent in seeking to apply the mysteries of cards and numbers to a divination of future events; all that he can scrape together goes to the lottery, in which he commenced by gaining one-third of a prize, and never succeeded in gaining anything since. He was a friend of Cagliostro and of the Count St. Germain, he pretends to belong to their society, and like them, professes to have in his possession the secret of the Elixir of Life. If you ask him his real age, he will tell you that it is two hundred and seventy-five years: he lived at first a hundred years, without any infirmity, from the reign of Henry II. to that of Louis XIV.; after that, thanks to his secret of the Elixir of Life, though apparently to the eyes of the vulgar he departed this life, he has accomplished three other ages of fifty years each. At the present moment he commences his fourth term of fifty years, and is only apparently fifty-five years of age. The first two hundred and fifty-five years are only counted in his own recollection. He will thus live, as he even publicly asserts, until the last day. In the fifth century we should have led Alliette to the stake—that would have been wrong; now-a-days we are content to pity him, and still we are wrong. Alliette is for all this one of the happiest men on the face of the earth; his talk is only of divination by cards, sorcery, De Tot's Egyptian science, or the Asiatic mysteries. He has published on all these subjects numerous little pamphlets, which nobody cares to read, but which, meanwhile, are put in type by some publisher, a greater fool than himself, and brought out under his anagram of Etteilla, or some other pseudonymic; indeed he has always his hat full of these absurd pamphlets. Do look at him now: see, he holds his hat firmly under his arm, as if he was afraid of losing some of his precious pamphlets. Take a survey of the man, look at his countenance; regard well his dress, and you will see that nature is always harmonious: you see the hat is of a piece with the head, the man with the clothes; his very doublet, as you romance writers would say, indicates the man."

In fact, nothing could be more true. I regarded Alliette attentively. He was dressed in a costume loose, ill-made, old fashioned, dusty, and stained; his hat, which looked as if made of green leather, was immoderately extended towards the top; he wore small clothes of black coarse woollen; black, or I should rather have said russet, stockings; and his shoes were rounded like those of the portraits of the kings in whose reign he pretended to have drawn breath.

As for his personal figure: he was a short thick-set man, with a countenance rugged, ill-favored and frayed, his mouth was large, toothless, and invested with a perpetual grimace; his hair was long, thin, and yellow, and fluttered round his head like a halo.

"He is talking to the Abbé Moulle," said I to M. Ledru: "who accompanied us in our affair of this morning: and it is that same occurrence which is the cause of the present meeting, is it not?"

"And why should that have given rise to our meeting here?" asked M. Ledru, looking at me with an inquisitive air.

"Because—but you will perhaps pardon me—you appeared to me to believe in the possibility of that unfortunate woman's head speaking after decapitation."

"Ah! ah! you seem to be a physiognomist. Well, well: it is true, I must own: yes, we have come hither to discuss the question. And if you are at all curious on such subjects, you will have an opportunity of hearing some opinions on them. But let us pass on to the Abbé Moulle."

"He must be," interrupted I, "a man of very engaging manners; for the softness of his voice, when he replied to the interrogatories of the commissary particularly struck me."

"Good—you are right again, this time. Moulle is a friend of mine of forty years' standing, and

he is only sixty himself. If you will observe, he is as neat, precise, and clean in his appearance and dress as Alliette is slovenly, dirty, and awkward. Moulle is a man of the world in the highest degree; and moves in the first ranks of society, in the Faubourg St. Germain: he it is who unites the sons and daughters of the peerage of France; and these marriages give him the opportunity of pronouncing on those interesting occasions those sweet little sermons which the contracting parties get printed and keep as precious family memorials. He ought to have been made Bishop of Clermont. Do you know the reason of his not attaining that dignity? I will tell you. It is because he has been for some time the friend of Cazotte: because that, like Cazotte latterly, he believes in the existence of inferior and superior spirits, of good and bad genii: like Alliette, he boasts a great collection of books, you will find in his library everything that has ever been written upon the subjects of visions, apparitions and spectres, upon hobgoblins, unquiet spirits, and imps of all kinds. Although he is very chary of speaking on any of those peculiar and heterodox subjects, except among intimate friends,—he is firmly convinced, discreet as he may be in avowing it, that everything which happens in this world is caused either by the puissance of some infernal agent, or by the intervention of some celestial intelligences. You will observe that he listens silently to that which Alliette is advancing, as if he was intent on looking at something which his companion sees nothing of, and to which he responds by a movement of the lips or a sign with his head. Sometimes, in the midst of us all, he will suddenly fall into a dark reverie—cold, trembling, and giddy, he walks to and fro in the saloon. In that case, the best plan is to leave him to himself: it might be, perhaps, dangerous to awaken him. I say awaken him, for I really believe him on such occasions to be in a fit of somnambulism. In most cases he awakens of himself, and, in that case, you will observe his conversation is very interesting after awakening."

"Oh, but tell me," said I to M. Ledru; "it appears to me that he has invoked one of those spirits of which you speak at this very moment?"

And I pointed out to my host a really spectral looking walker, who now rejoined the two gentlemen conversing, and who took great pains to be careful of putting his foot down betwixt the flowers, though it was evident to me that he had room enough to walk straight along without touching them.

"That gentleman," said M. Ledru to me, "is another friend of mine: Le Chevalier Lenoire."

"The founder of the Museum of the Petits-Augustins?"

"The very same. He is dying of chagrin for the dispersion of his Museum, for which he, from '92 to '94, was a dozen times within an hair's breadth of being killed. The Restoration, with its customary love for the intellectual, shut it up; and gave orders that the monuments should be restored to the edifices from which they had been originally taken, or to the families who had a right to reclaim them. Unfortunately, the greater portion of the monuments had been

"Ah! ah! The chart of affection."—*Page* 17.

destroyed—most of the families were extinct—consequently the most curious specimens of our antique sculpture, and of course, memorials of our national history, have been dispersed—lost. It is ever thus with what relates to old France: there remain now only its fragments—and of these in a very short period nothing will be left. And who are they who have destroyed them? who—but the men who ought to have the greatest interest in their preservation."

And M. Ledru, ultra-liberal as he was, at this epoch, sighed deeply.

"Are those the whole of my fellow-guests?" asked I of M. Ledru.

"We may perhaps have the company of Dr. Robert. I can say nothing of him: I presume you will judge for yourself. He is a man who has been through a long life perpetually engaged in making experiments on the human frame, just as one might cut and hack an image, without the least scruple or doubts as to whether the human frame thus subjected to his experiments had a soul to be affected by sorrow, or nerves to be tortured by pain. He is a jolly fellow, and a boon companion: but no man perhaps has killed so many of his fellow-creatures. But, happily for him, he has no faith in ghosts. His mind is of a very common order: which leads him to believe that because he is a noisy fellow he is intellectual: because he is an atheist, he fancies himself a great philosopher. He is one of those men whom we receive, not that we wish for their company, but because they will come to our house. As for seeking them in their own houses, such an idea would never present itself to one's mind."

"It was a lady, sitting in the shadow of a bower of vines."—*Page* 22.

"Oh, my good sir, I have known several of this species."

"We ought to have had another friend of mine, rather younger than Alliette, than the Abbé Moulle, or the Chevalier Lenoire, who will sometimes take a part in conversation with M. Alliette on his science of divination,—with Moulle on his demonology, with Lenoire on antiquities: he is a living library: a catalogue bound in a Christian skin,—but you ought to know him well yourself."

"You mean the bibliopolist Jacob?"

"Precisely."

"And will he not be here?"

"He has not as yet made his appearance: and as he is aware of our dining ordinarily at two o'clock, and it wants but a quarter of an hour to that time, it is not very likely that he will be here at all. He is at present deeply engaged in search of some rare old book, printed at Amsterdam in 1570, the first edition of which has three typographical errors, one in the title, one in the seventh page, and another in the last page."

At that moment the door of the saloon opened, and Mother Antoine appeared, announcing that dinner was served.

"Come, gentlemen," said M. Ledru, opening in his turn the door which led to the garden, and addressing the promenading guests, "to table! to table." Then turning towards me, he said:

"Now, my friend, there is in another part of the garden,—besides those your fellow-guests of whom I have given you those historical details— a person that you have never yet seen, and of whom I have not spoken to you. The lady is too much detached from the common affairs of this world to have heard the call which I just made to our friends to come to table, and which, as you can see, have quickly brought them here. Go now and look about you: When you shall have found this immateriality, this transparent evanescence, *eine Erscheinung;** as they say in German, you must try to persuade her that it is good to eat sometimes, if not to live: you, in fact, will offer her your arm, and bring her with you to table. Now go."

I obeyed M. Ledru, guessing that this charming spirit I was going to look for would afford me an agreeable surprise; and I quickly stepped forth into the garden, and cast my eyes inquiringly around me. My search for the fair one was short, for almost immediately I caught sight of what I was seeking for.

It was a lady, sitting in the shade of a bower of vines, of whom I could see neither her countenance nor her height. I could see nothing of the first, for it was turned towards the open country: of the other because she was enveloped in a large shawl. But I could see she was dressed in black.

I approached close to her without her making the least movement, the noise of my footsteps had evidently failed to reach her ear. She was as immoveable as a statue; all that I could now perceive was that she was of a fine and distinguished figure. I had already perceived that she was fair; and a gleam of sunshine, passing through the trellices of the vines, played upon her hair, giving it the appearance of a golden halo. I could thus remark the beautiful fineness of her hair, which rivalled those silky threads which the first autumnal breezes detach from the harvest-thistle; her neck—a little too long, perhaps, by-the-by, a charming fault, inasmuch as it adds almost invariably an additional grace, if it is not a point of beauty—her neck was beautifully arched and her head was sppported by her right hand, the elbow of which rested on the back of her chair, while her left hand hung negligently by her side, holding a white rose at the extremity of her tapering fingers. Swan-like neck, folded hand, drooping arm—all was of the same dead white—I might indeed say they seemed to be of Parian marble, a veinless surface, a pulseless interior: the rose, which had already began to fade, had more of colour and of life than the hand that held it.

I gazed at her for a moment, the more I gazed the conviction stole over me that it could not be a living being that was before my eyes. So firm was this feeling that I hesitated for a moment whether I should address her, or return without doing so. Twice or thrice my lips opened—but without having pronounced a syllable; at last I decided I would speak.

"Madame," said I.

She started, and turning herself round, looked at me with astonishment, as if she had been in a sort of dream, from which I had suddenly recalled her wandering thoughts.

Her large black eyes fixed on me—for notwithstanding her fair hair, as I have described, she had eyebrows and eyes as dark as night—

her large black eyes were fixed on me with a strange expression.

She was a woman of about thirty-two or three years of age; she must have been possessed of wonderful beauty ere her cheeks had hollowed, or her colour faded: her features were of the same pearly whiteness as her arms and hands, without the slightest tinge of blood in them: this contrast made her eyes appear jet—her lips coral.

"Madame," repeated I, "M. Ledru has empowered me to inform you that I am the author of *Henry III.*, of *Christine*, and of *Antony;* would you have the kindness to consider me as presented, and accept my arm as far as the dining-room."

"Pardon me, sir," said she, "you have been here some few moments, have you not? I felt that you were present, but I had no power to turn round: it happens thus to me sometimes when I have my gaze directed towards a certain direction. Your voice, however, has broken the charm. Give me your arm: we will go."

She rose, and passed her arm under mine; but though there was no appearance of constraint in her manner, I could scarcely feel the pressure of her arm. It was as if a shadow was walking by my side.

We reached the dining-room: neither of us having said a word to each other on the way.

Two places were reserved at the table: one on the right of M. Ledru for the lady: one opposite the lady for myself.

CHAPTER V.

MYSTERY II.—THE EXECUTIONER AND CHARLOTTE CORDAY.

In strict harmony with everything else appertaining to the abode of M. Ledru, the dining-table had its own peculiarities and distinctive character.

Its shape was that of an immense horse-shoe, the two ends resting on the windows of the garden, leaving three-fourths of the immense room free for the service. This table could well accommodate twenty persons, and that without the least inconvenience or cramping; here they always dined, whether M. Ledru had one, two, four, ten, or twenty guests: to-day we numbered six only, and we could hardly cover one-third of the table.

Every Tuesday the same bill of fare was presented. M. Ledru thought that, during the other days of the week, his guests might eat of anything they liked at their own houses, or whatever they might chance to get at other people's, but on Tuesdays there were invariably laid on M. Ledru's table, soup, beef, *poulets à l'estragon*, roast leg of mutton, haricots and a sallad. The pullets were duplicate, or triplicate, varying according to the number or tastes of his guests.

Whatever the number or however few his guests, or even if alone, M. Ledru seated himself at one of the ends of the table, his back to the garden, his face to the court. He sat in an old arm-chair, which had seemed to have grown into its position from having been for the last ten years in the same place. Here he received from the hands of his gardener Antoine, metamorphosed on such occasions into a footman, not only the table-wine, but some bottles of old Burgundy which were brought to him with a religious respect, and which M. Ledru drew and handed round to his guests with a care and reverence not at all inferior to that of his gardener-footman.

At twenty-eight we do believe in some things: ten years later, we believe in nothing : not even in old wine.

The dinner passed off as most dinners do : we praised the cookery, and lauded the wine. The young lady, however, contented herself with eating some crumbs of bread, and drinking one glass of water ; she never breathed a syllable. By Jove ! she recalled to my mind the horrible story of the goule in the Arabian Nights, who, when at table with her husband, amused herself by eating rice with a toothpick.

After dinner we passed into the saloon for coffee. It was natural for me to give my arm to our silent guest. Indeed, she came half-way to take it. There was always the same languor in her movements, the same grace in her motions and manner, I was almost going to say the same impalpability in her limbs.

I conducted the lady to a sofa on which she reclined.

Meanwhile, two persons had, whilst we were dining, been introduced into the saloon. They were the Doctor and the Commissary of Police.

The Commissary had come to get our signatures attached to the *procès-verbal*, which the murderer Jacquemin had already signed in the prison.

A slight trace of blood was visible on the paper as he presented it to me. On signing it, I said : " Whence comes this spot ? Is it the blood of the female or her husband ?"

" It comes," said the Commissary, "from a wound that the murderer has in his hand, and the continued bleeding of which we could not stop."

" Have you learnt, M. Ledru," said the Doctor, " that this brute persists in his assertion that the head of his victim spoke to him after decapitation ?"

" And you believe the thing to be impossible—is it not so, Doctor ?"

" *Parbleu !* I do."

" You believe it also to be impossible that the eyes should open after the head is separated from the trunk ?"

" It is impossible."

" Then you do not believe that the blood, interrupted in its escape by the bed of plaster, which stopped immediately the efflux from the arteries and veins, could have given back to the head a moment of life and feeling ?"

" I believe nothing of the sort."

" Very well," said M. Ledru, " but for myself I do believe it possible."

" And I," said Alliette.

" I also," said the Abbé Moule.

" So do I," said the Chevalier Lenoire.

" I also," said I.

The Commissary of Police and the White Lady were the only persons who did not respond : doubtless, the one because the subject had not sufficient interest for him : the other because it might be that the subject had too much of interest in it.

" Ah ! if you are at all against me, you ought to have good reasons. Still, if one of you were a medical man."

" But, doctor," said M. Ledru, " you know that I have some pretensions that way."

" In that case," said the doctor, " you ought to know that in the instance alluded to there can be no more of pain—there is an end to all feeling : and that the sentient power is destroyed by the section of the vertebral chord."

" And who told you so ?" asked M. Ledru.

" My reason,—what else ?"

" Oh ! very finely answered indeed ! Was it not also the same reason which informed the judges who condemned Galileo, that the sun turned round the earth, and that the latter was a motionless body ? Reason is often a fool, my dear doctor. Have you yourself made any experiments on heads after decapitation ?"

" No—never."

" Have you read Sommering's dissertations ? Have you read the minutes of Doctor Sue ? Have you perused Dr. Ollcher's protest ?"

" No."

" So—you believe, do you not, simply upon the report of M. Guillotin, that his machine is the most rapid, the most certain, and the least painful means of destroying life ?"

" I do believe it."

" Well, you are mistaken, my dear friend."

" Ah !—but the proofs ?"

" Listen, Doctor : since you have made an appeal to science, I will speak of science : and not one here, I can well believe, is so much a stranger to it, that he will be debarred from taking a part in the discussion."

The doctor made a gesture as if he doubted the assertion.

" No matter : in that case you will have the subject all to yourself."

We drew our seats nearer towards M. Ledru: and, for my own part, I listened most attentively : for t his question of the comparative pangs of death, whether produced by the operation of the cord, the steel, or poison, had often occurred to my mind as a question of humanity. Indeed I had myself made some researches on the subject of the agonies which precede, accompany, and follow the infliction of the different popular modes of capital punishment.

" Say on"—said the doctor in an incredulous tone.

" It is easy to demonstrate to any one possessing the scantiest notion of the construction of the vital powers of the human body," continued M. Ledru, " that the sentient powers are not entirely and immediately destroyed by the punishment alluded to ; and this which I now advance is founded, not upon questionable hypothesis, but undeniable facts."

" Show us your facts."

" Here they are. In the first place, the seat of sensation or feeling, is it not located in the brain ?"

" Very probably."

" The operations of this consciousness of feeling

Dr. Robert.

may be carried on, even whilst the circulation of blood through the brain is arrested, enfeebled, or partially destroyed."

"It is possible."

If then the seat of the faculty of sensation is in the brain, as long as the brain retains its vital powers, the sufferer has a knowledge of its existence."

"But the proofs—the proofs ?"

"There they are. Haller, in his Elements of Medical Science," vol. 4. p. 35, says :—

"A head, after being separated from the body, opened its eyes, and looked askance at me, the instant that, with the tip of my finger I had pressed the spinal marrow."

"Haller : be it so. But Haller has deceived himself."

"If he has deceived himself, I am content to let it be. Then we will pass on to another. Weycard, in his Philosophy of Arts, p. 221, says :

"I have seen the lips of a man move after his head had been struck off."

"Good. But did they move so as to speak ?"

"Listen. We shall come to that. What says Sommering—his works are open on the table, and you can see for yourself ?—Sommering says :—

"Many medical men, colleagues of mine, have assured me that they have seen human heads, after having been separated from the body, grind their teeth as if in agony ; and I am myself fully convinced that if circulation of air through the organs of the voice be retained, the head may actually speak."

The discussion.—*Page 26.*

"And now, doctor," continued M. Ledru, and he grew pale as he spoke, "I will go farther than Sommering. I—I myself have heard the head of a human being articulate after de-capitation!"

We all started up. The pale lady even raised herself from the sofa on which she had reclined.

"You?"

"Yes—I. Will you tell me also that I am a fool?"

"*Dame!*" said the doctor, "if you tell me that you have yourself——"

"Yes, I tell you that I have indeed seen and heard the thing come to pass. You are too polite, I have not the least doubt, doctor, to tell me plainly to my face that I am foolish, but I am well aware you believe so in your own mind, and that amounts in the end to the same thing."

"Oh, well! go on: relate to us the affair." said the doctor.

"That is a very easy word for you to say. Know, then, that this which you ask me to relate to you—to you, of all men—I have never revealed to any living being during the thirty-seven years which have elapsed since the oc-currence. Know, then, that I would not guarantee that I should not faint in the recital of it, as I fainted at the moment that gory head spoke to me—when its dying eyes were fixed on mine in hopeless agony."

The conversation became at this point more and more interesting: the situation increased in dramatic effect.

"Go on, Ledru: take courage," said Alliette, "and tell us the story."

"Pray, recount the affair, my friend," said the Abbé Moulle.

"Do tell it us?" said the Chevalier Lenoire.

"Monsieur—" murmured the pale lady.

I said nothing, but the wish to hear it might be seen in my eyes.

"It is strange," said M. Ledru, without answering, but as if speaking to himself, "it is strange what influence these events exercise upon us all. You all know me well?" said M. Ledru, turning himself to the side where I was seated.

"I know, sir, that you are a gentleman well-educated, very intellectual; that you give splendid dinners, and that you are mayor of Fontenay-aux-Roses."

M. Ledru smiled, as he thanked me by bowing to me, and said—

"But I mean as to my origin—my family."

"I am, indeed, sir, ignorant of your origin, and I do not know your family."

"Well, listen, I am going to speak of them to you—and perhaps I may, after I have done so, narrate to you the tale you so much desire to hear. If it is forthcoming—good; it will be for you to take it as it is given; if it is withheld, I pray you not to persist in asking for it.

Every one present seated themselves in a way the most comfortable for listening.

Few places could have been so well suited for the recital of the horrible or lugubrious, as the saloon in which we were assembled. Vast in its extent, the large thick curtains obscured the feeble light of the fast deepening twilight, the angles of the room were settled in deep gloom, and the only things plainly distinguishable in the obscurity were the lines marking the doors and windows opening into the garden.

In one of the darkest of these gloomy corners sat the pale lady: her black dress was completely absorbed in the surrounding darkness, and nothing of her was visible but her pale face and amber hair, immoveable and thrown back on the sofa cushion.

M. Ledru began thus:—

"I am," said he, "a son of the famous Comus, physician to Louis XVI. and Marie-Antoinette. My father whose burlesque surname has unfortunately classed him among the jugglers and charlatans of the day, was a scientific man, and highly distinguished in the schools of Volta, of Galvani, and of Mesmer. He was the first in France who occupied himself in the pursuit of phantasmagorical and electrical science; giving metaphysical and mathematical lectures at court.

"The unhappy and unfortunate Marie-Antoinette, whom I have seen a score of times, and who more than once has taken me in her arms and kissed me, whilst I was a child—that is, on her first arrival in France—poor Marie-Antoinette was excessively pleased with my father's talents; and Joseph II., on his departure from Paris in 1777, declared that he had seen nothing more worthy of seeing in France than Comus.

"In the midst of these occupations and pursuits, my father found time to attend to the education of my brother and myself. Consequently, we were initiated in a knowledge of occult science, and a number of facts and experiments in galvanism, magnetism, and such like knowledge, were explained and made known to us, facts which are now-a-days public property, but which, at the period of which I am speaking, were things hidden from the multitude, and only known by a select few. In 1793, the mere circumstance of my father having been state physician, made him a prisoner; but, thanks to some friendships I had formed among the chiefs of the party of the Mountain, I obtained his release. After this, my father retired to this very house, in which he died in 1807, at the age of sixty-six.

"I will now revert to myself; I have said that I had formed friendships with the men of the Mountain. In fact, I was intimately connected with Danton and Camille Desmoulins. Marat I knew, but more in the quality of a doctor than a friend. The result of these friendships, short as they were in point of duration, was, that on the day when they dragged Charlotte Corday to the scaffold, I resolved to be present at her execution."

"I can go thus far with you," said I, "in aid of your discussion with Doctor Robert as to the retention of life, as to be able to narrate to you the historical facts relative to Charlotte Corday."

"We shall come to that very shortly," interrupted M. Ledru, "pray let me continue. I am a living witness of the fact: and for that reason what I now recount to you, you can the more readily believe.

"At two o'clock in the morning I took my station close by the statue of Liberty. It was a hot, sultry, lowering July morning, the sky was overcast, and there was every indication of the approach of a summer storm.

"At four o'clock the storm descended: at that same moment, as I have been informed, Charlotte emerged from her prison and ascended the cart.

"They had come to take her from prison to the scaffold at the very moment that a young painter was engaged in taking her portrait. Death seemed thus jealously determined that nothing of this young girl should survive—not even her semblance. The artist had made his first rough sketch of the head, and, strange to say, was occupied in drawing the outline of the neck—in fact, had reached the point where the axe of the guillotine should first meet the fair and living flesh beneath it—when the executioner entered.

"The lightning flashed, the rain fell in torrents, and the thunder reverbrated in the heavens: but all failed to disperse the curious and anxious crowd around the scaffold. The quays, the bridges, the squares, the approaches were filled with a dense compact mass of human beings; the cries and murmurs and groans of this immense body of people nearly overwhelmed the mutterings of the thunder. Females, who were designated by the opprobrious, but perhaps not too strong term of guillotine-lickers,*—such their infuriate, insatiate thirst for bloodshed—hurled aloud their maledictions. I could hear

* Lecheuses guillotines.

their cries and execrations increase as one would approach the thunders of a cataract. Long before I could perceive the approach of anything, I could perceive the populace undulating like the waves of some agitated ocean; at last, like some unfortunate ship, tossed and swayed here and there by the howling and tumultuous waves, the cart appeared, labouring, straining—now seen—now hidden amid that hellish sea—and I could finally see the features of the condemned woman—whom I had never before seen—should never again see.

"She was a very beautiful young woman of about twenty-seven years of age; her eyes were magnificent; her nose finely formed; and lips beautifully modelled: she stood upright: her head uplifted—not from a desire to appear to despise the mob which surrounded her, but from the fact of her hands being tied behind her, rendering such a position inevitable. The rain had now ceased; but as for three quarters of an hour she had been exposed to its fury, her garments clung close to her, and revealed the outlines of a form god-like in symmetry and loveliness; she looked truly as if she had just emerged from the bath. The red robe with which she had been invested by the executioner gave a strange aspect—an awful splendor—to that head so proudly elevated—those features so full of energy. At the moment of her arrival at the foot of the scaffold, a ray of sunshine escaping from betwixt two heavy dull masses of clouds, played among her hair, investing it with a sudden splendor which seemed to give her the appearance of being surrounded by a halo of light. In good faith, I can avow to you, though I knew that this young girl was a murderess—that she had been guilty of an atrocious crime which humanity was bound to avenge—I say to you, that however I might have detested the crime, I could not at that moment have told you whether I was being present at the apotheosis of a saint, or the execution of a criminal. On perceiving the scaffold, the color left her cheeks; and this pallor was the more remarkable, from the contrast of her red robe, which reached to her neck: but almost immediately afterwards she recovered her firmness by a strong effort of will, and turning herself to the scaffold, looked at it and smiled.

The cart stopped. Charlotte jumped lightly to the ground, without permitting any one to assist her in descending from the vehicle, and mounted the steps of the scaffold,—now glistening and slippery from the recent rain,—as fast as the length of her robe which trailed on the ground, and her bound hands, would permit. When she felt the executioner place his hands upon her shoulder for the purpose of withdrawing the handkerchief which covered her neck, a second time was perceptible, that sudden pallor of countenance I have before alluded to—but almost instantaneously she recovered herself by a smile; and she, with a quick and almost lively motion, escaped the infamy of being tied to the fatal board, by putting her head through the hideous aperture. Swiftly glided the knife down the groove, and the head, detached from the trunk, fell on and rebounded from the platform. It was then,—I pray you listen well to me, doctor,

and you, sir poet,—it was then that one of the attendants on the executioner, named Legros, seized the head by its hair, and inspired with a vile wish to gratify the brutality of the mob, gave it a smart slap on the cheek. Well—I swear to you that at this blow given on the face, the head was suffused with a blush of indignation—a color not perceptible on one cheek alone—understand me well—I saw that head blush—redden—not on the spot where the blow fell only—but with a regular color from brow to chin: I am fully assured that the sensation of feeling existed in that head after decapitation; that she felt and reddened with indignation at suffering a vile indignity which she could not resent.

"The populace saw this, as well as myself; and taking the part of the dead against the living, they with loud and ferocious cries, demanded instant vengeance on the executioner for the outrage committed: and forthwith the miserable wretch was handed over to the care of the gendarmes and conducted to prison.

"Pray wait a few moments," said M. Ledru to the Doctor, seeing he was about to interrupt him, "I have not yet told you all."

"I had a great desire to know what could have induced this man to act in the infamous manner he had done. I therefore made inquiries as to where they had taken him; and having obtained the information, and a permission to visit him in prison, I repaired to l'Abbaye, where they had shut him up.

A decree of the Revolutionary Tribunal had condemned him to three months' incarceration. He could not understand how it was that he had been thus sentenced for the commission of an act so *natural* as that which he had done.

"I asked him what were his reasons for striking the deceased.

"'Don't ask such a silly question. I am a Maratist—I am. It was my duty to punish her on the account of the law: it was my will to punish on my own account.'

"'But,' said I, 'can you not comprehend that the violation of respect due to the dead is in itself a great wrong—if not a crime?'

"'Ah! then,' said Legros to me, looking at me fixedly, 'you believe they die instantly on beheading them—don't you?'

"'Doubtless.'

"'Ah!—one may easily know you have never had a peep into the basket where they are all put together; that *you* have never seen them, as I have, roll their eyes and grind their teeth for five minutes after being guillotined. Why we are obliged to get new baskets every two or three months—so much are they injured by the teeth of the condemned. You see it is a heap of aristocratic heads—who can never make up their minds to die; and, *parbleu*, I should not at all be surprised if one of them should cry out 'Vive le Roi.'

"I knew as much as I wished to know from him: so I left the prison: but left it, eternally harassed by one idea—that human heads lived after being guillotined—and I internally resolved to satisfy myself of its truth or falsehood."

———

"Ah! you believe they die instantly on beheading them, don't you."—*Page* 27.

CHAPTER VI.

MYSTERY III.—ALBERT AND SOLANGE.

Night had completely set in during the recital of M. Ledru's narrative. The occupants of the room could be discerned only as dim shadows—mute and motionless—motionless from anxiety lest M. Ledru would here end his recital: for they well comprehended, that, terrible as was the tale just related, there was more in store for lovers of the horrible in that which was as yet untold.

Not a whisper was to be heard. The Doctor alone opened his mouth as if to speak, when I seized him by the arm to hinder him from breaking the silence ; and he refrained.

After the pause of a few seconds, M. Ledru continued :

"I departed from the prison and crossed the Place Taranne on my way to Rue de Tournons, in which street I lodged, when I heard a female voice calling loudly for succour.

"The lateness of the hour—now almost ten o'clock at night—convinced me that the cry could not have come from the criminals ; so I ran towards the corner of the square from whence the voice was heard, and I saw, by the light of the moon now suddenly emerging from the clouds, a woman struggling in the midst of a party of revolutionary *sans-culottes*.

Solange.

The woman instantly catching sight of me, and perceiving from my dress that it was not altogether that of 'a man of the people,' she ran quickly towards me, crying out:

"'Ah! here! here is the very M. Albert who knows me well. He will tell you that I am really the daughter of Mother Lédieu, the laundress.'

"So saying, the poor woman, pale and trembling, seized me by the arm and clung to me like a drowning man to the plank which would save him.

"'Thou mayest be the daughter of Mother Lédieu for aught we care, but thou hast not the card of citizenship, my fine maid, and therefore thou must follow us to the guard-house!'

"The young woman tightened her grasp of my arm, and in that firm pressure I could feel embodied her terror of death, and her prayer for help combined. I understood it all.

"As it was evident that she had called me by the first name that presented itself to her agitated mind, I, in like manner, addressed her by that which came most readily to my memory.

"'What! is it you, my poor Solange!' said I to her, 'what has happened to you?'

"'There—do you see, gentlemen,' replied the woman to her captors.

"It appears to me that thou speakest very much like an aristocrat, citizeness."

"'Listen to me, Mr. Sergeant, it is not at all my fault that I speak as I do,' said the young girl, 'my mother's custom lay all among grand people; and she consequently taught me to be very polite to her customers, so that it is merely a bad habit which I have been taught: but you will readily see, Mr. Sergeant, that I cannot get rid of it all at once.'

"And in making this answer, in a voice trembling with terror and anxiety, there was an under-current of raillery which was imperceptible to all but myself. I asked myself the question—Who can this young girl be? but the problem was too much for me to resolve. All that I was sure of was this—she was no laundress's daughter.

"'You ask me what is the matter, citizen Albert!' said the girl: 'I will tell you all about it. You must understand that I came out to-day to carry home some linen: when I reached my destination, the mistress of the house was not at home: so I waited until she came back to receive my payment. *Dame!* in these days every one wants his money as soon as he can get it. Well: night came on: I had intended to have reached home by day, and therefore did not take my card of citizenship with me. I fell in on my way home with these gentlemen—I really beg pardon—I should have said citizens; they demanded my card: I told them I had not got it with me; they wished to conduct me to the guard-house. I cried out; you ran to help me: we mutually recognised each other. Then I was reassured: and I said to myself, Now, as M. Albert knows that my name is Solange—as he knows that I am the daughter of Mother Lédieu, the laundress, he will answer for me. Is it not so, Monsieur Albert?'

"'Certainly—I will answer for you, and I do answer.'

"'Good!' said the chief of the patrol, 'and who is to be answerable for thee, my fine fellow?'

"'Danton. Will you go to him? He is a good patriot—is he not?'

"'Oh! if Danton will answer for thee, there is nothing more to be said.'

"'Well thought of: to-day the Cordeliers sit—will you go as far as that?'

"'We will go that far. Citizens sans-culottes, forward, march!'

"The club of the Cordeliers at that time held their sittings in the old convent of the Cordeliers, rue de l'Observance: we were at the spot almost instantaneously. On our reaching the entrance I tore a blank leaf from my pocket book, wrote a few words on it in pencil, and gave it to the sergeant with a request that he himself would carry it to Danton, while we remained in the custody of the corporal and the rest of the patrol.

"The sergeant went into the club, and came out with Danton.

"'What!' said he on seeing me, 'is it thou they have arrested—thou, my best friend!—thou, the friend of Camille! thou, who art one of the best republicans that ever breathed! Go to, citizen sergeant,' added he, turning to the chief of the patrol, "I will be responsible for him. Will that do?'

"'Thou wilt be responsible for him; but who will be responsible for her?' asked the pertinacious sergeant.

"'For her? Of whom speakest thou?'

"'Of this woman—who else?'

"'For him, and for her, for all that may be with him; will that content thee?'

"'Yes, I am perfectly satisfied—above all,' said the sergeant, 'with having seen thee.'

"'Ah, by Jove! thou can'st give thyself that pleasure gratis: take thy fill of it whilst I am here to be seen.'

"'Thanks! Continue to advocate as thou hast done the people's interests, and rest thyself assured they will ever acknowledge thy services.'

"'Ah! yes—I rely on that, above all,' said Danton.

"'Would'st thou give me a shake of thy hand?' asked the sergeant.

"'Why not?' And Danton gave him his hand.

"'*Vive Danton!*' cried the sergeant.

"'*Vive Danton!*' repeated the patrol in chorus, as they left the building, conducted by their chief, who, after having walked off some ten paces, again returned, threw up his red bonnet in the air, again vociferating "*Vive Danton!*" the cry again re-echoed by his followers.

"I stepped back to thank Danton, whilst his name, incessantly repeated from the interior of the building, reached even where we stood. 'Danton! Danton!' cried the members, 'to the tribune!' 'Pardon me, my dear friend,' said he, 'thou hearest this appeal,—one shake of the hand, and leave me to re-enter the hall. I have given the right hand to the sergeant,—thou shalt have the left. Who knows, the worthy patriot might have the itch?'

"So saying, he returned into the interior, exclaiming, in that powerful voice which had so often overborne and calmed the outbursts of popular street commotions, 'Behold me—here am I.'

"I was left at the door with my fair unknown.

"'Now madam,' said I to the lady, 'where shall I conduct you? I am at your service.'

"'Of course—to Mother Lédieu the laundress's,' she replied, laughing, 'you know very well she is my mamma.'

"'But where does Mamma Lédieu live?'

"'Rue Férou, No. 24.'

"'Well then, we will hasten to Mother Lédieus', rue Férou, No. 24.'

"We retraced our steps to the rue des Fossés-Monsieur-le-Prince, as far as the rue des Fossés-Saint-Germain; afterwards traversed the rue du Petit-Lion, then went up the place Saint-Sulpice, then the rue Férou.

"All this portion of our road was past without a word being interchanged on either side. I occupied myself, thanks to a brilliant moonlight now shining in uninterrupted splendor, in examining at my ease the features of my companion.

"She was indeed a lovely woman, probably from twenty to twenty-two years of age, a brunette, with large blue eyes, with far more of the intellectual than the grave in their expression; with a nose finely cut and classical in its outline, pouting saucy lips, teeth like pearls, the hands of a queen, the feet of a child, and above all, under the vulgar costume of Mother Lédieu's daughter, there still was that aristocratical bearing and grace, which had, and with good reason for it, awakened the suspicion of the obstinate sergeant of the revolutionary patrol.

"On our arrival at No. 24, we stopped and gazed at each other for a moment in silence.

"'Well : what is it you wish to say, my dear Monsieur Albert ?' said the unknown to me, smiling as she asked the question.

"'I wish to say, my dear Mademoiselle Solange, that it is a great vexation to me to have met with you only to leave you again so quickly.'

"'But I really must beg a thousand pardons. I find that it is no vexation at all, but quite the contrary : for understand that if I had not encountered you, they would have infallibly taken me off to the guard-house ; they would have found out that I was not Mother Lédieu's daughter ; they would have discovered that I was an aristocrat, and there is every probability that the affair would have finished in my losing my head.'

"'You avow then that you are an aristocrat ?'

"'I—I avow nothing !'

"'But at least you will let me know your name ?'

"'Solange.'

"'You are well aware that that name, which I gave you on the spur of the moment, is not your right name ?'

"'No matter : I love it, and I shall keep it—for yourself, at all events.'

"'What necessity will you have to keep it for me, if I am never to see you again.'

"'I do not say that ; I merely say that if we should meet again, it would be just as useless for you to know my name as for me to know yours. I called you Albert : keep your name of Albert, as I shall keep that of Solange.'

"'Well—be it so : but listen, Solange,' said I to her.

"'I am listening, Albert,' replied she.

"'You are an aristocrat—you admit it.'

"'If I were not to admit, you would guess it, would you not ? so, my admission would lose much of its merit !'

"'And being an aristocrat you have been persecuted ?'

"'You are, indeed, not far from the truth !'

"'And you hide yourself to avoid your persecutors ?'

"'Rue Fèrou, 24, at Mother Ledieu's, whose husband was my father's coachman. You see I have no secret for you !'

"'And your father ?'

"'I have indeed no secrets for you, my dear Monsieur Albert, so long as they are mine : but my father's secrets are not mine to divulge. My father is hidden somewhere near the coast, waiting for the opportunity to emigrate. And now you know all that I can tell you.'

"'And you—what do you intend to do ?'

"'Emigrate with my father, if possible : but if that cannot be done, he will go alone, and leave me to follow him.'

"'And to-night, when you were arrested, you were returning from a visit to your father.'

"'I was.'

"'Listen to me, dear Solange.'

"'I am listening to you.'

"'You have watched the events of this night ?'

"'Yes : and from it I have learnt to estimate the extent of your influence.'

"'As to that, my influence is not very great, unfortunately. But, nevertheless, I have some friends.'

"'I have to-night obtained a knowledge of one of them ?'

"'And you know well he is a man not altogether powerless at this epoch.'

"'Do you think of employing his influence in aiding my father's escape.'

"'No : I have reserved that for yourself.'

"'And for my father—'

"'As for your father, I have another means.'

"'You have another means !' exclaimed Solange, clasping my hands, and looking me in the face with an expression of intense anxiety.

"'If I save your father, will you not cherish a good thought of me ?'

"'My life shall be one whole feeling of gratitude for your kindness.' She pronounced these words with an ineffable expression of anticipated gratitude and love. Then, in a supplicating tone, she asked—'and will that be a sufficient recompense ?'

"'Yes,' I answered.

"'Thank Heaven, I was not deceived : you have indeed a noble heart. I thank you sincerely, in the name of my father and for myself ; and, even if success should fail you in the future, I am not a whit the less your debtor for the past.'

"'When may I again see you, Solange ?'

"'Whenever you have a wish to see me.'

"'To-morrow I hope to have some good news to tell you.'

"'Good ; we will see each other to-morrow.'

"'Where, then ?'

"'Here, if you like.'

"'Here—in the street ?'

"'Ah ! mon Dieu ! you may see that this is the surest place : during the past quarter of an hour that we have been conversing at this door, not a soul has passed.'

"'Why not let me enter your residence ; or why not come yourself to mine ?'

"'Because that, if you were to come into my house, it might compromise the good man who has given me an asylum : and if I were to go to your house, I might be the means of compromising you.'

"'Very well : be it as you say. I will take the card of one of my relatives, and I will give it to you.'

"'Worse. In that case your relative might be guillotined, if I should happen to be arrested.'

"'You are right indeed. I will bring you then a card in the name of Solange.'

"'The very thing ! You will see that my real and only name will turn out to be Solange, after all.'

"'At what hour ?'

"'The same hour at which we met to-day. At ten o'clock, if you please.'

"'Let it be ten.'

"'And how will you manage to meet me ?'

"'Oh, that will be easy enough. At five minutes to ten you must be at the door : at ten o'clock I will come down to you.'

"'Then, to-morrow, at ten, dear Solange.'

"'To-morrow, at ten, dear Albert.'

"I took her hand, and was about to kiss it ; she presented her brow to my lips.

The itinerant venders of the daily List of Condemned issued by the Revolutionary Tribunal in 1793.

"The next night, I was at the rendezvous at half-past nine o'clock. At a quarter to ten, Solange emerged from the door. Each of us had anticipated the hour of meeting.

"'I see that you have brought me some good news,' said she, smiling, as I bounded towards her.

"'Excellent: in the first place, I bring you your card.'

"'But in the first place—my father?' she inquired, putting back the hand which held the card.'

"'Your father is saved, if he wishes.'

"'If he wishes to be saved, you say : how could he do otherwise ?'

"'Then he must place confidence in me.'

"'He has already done that.'

"'You have seen him ?'

"'Yes.'

"'You run too great a risk by thus exposing yourself to observation.'

"'What would you have me do ? it was necessary : but God protected me.'

"'And so you told your father all that I said to you ?'

"'I told him that you had saved my life yesterday ; and would perhaps save his life to-morrow.'

"'To-morrow, yes : to-morrow, if he so will it. I will save him.'

"'How so—tell me—speak ! Oh ! what a happy meeting will ours have been, if it leads to such success.'

"'But there is one thing,' said I, and hesitated.

"'What ?'

"'You cannot go with him.'

"Look for me in the ruc Féron at this hour to-morrow."—*Page* 34.

"As to that, my mind is made up," she replied.

"Besides, at a future day, I am certain of being able to provide you with a passport."

"Speak of my father in the first place—we can speak of myself afterwards."

"Good! I told you I had friends—did I not?"

"Yes."

"Yesterday I visited one of them: his name is Marceau."

"General Marceau?"

"Exactly."

"If he has given his word, he will keep it."

"Well—he has promised."

"My God! how happy you have made me. Do tell me what he has promised."

"He has promised to aid us."

"In what way?"

"Oh, very simply. Kleber is coming to nominate him General in chief of the Army of the West; and he will leave here to-morrow night. Your father will go with him as his secretary. On his arrival in Vendée, Marceau will require your father's word of honour not to serve against France, and, the next night, he will be in the Vendéan camp; from thence on to Bretany—then to England. As soon as he is somewhat settled in London, he will write, I shall then procure you a passport, and you will rejoin him."

"My father must be informed of it."

"Certainly."

"To night?"

"Yes."

"But how—at this hour?"

"You shall take my card," said I, giving it her. Placing the card in her bosom, she took my arm, and we went as far as the Place Taranne at the spot where I had first encountered the watch.

"Wait for me here," said she, as she disappeared at the corner of the old Hotel Matignon. In a quarter of an hour she returned.

"Come," said she, "my father wishes to see and thank you."

Again taking my arm, she conducted me to a house in the rue Saint-Guillaume, opposite the hotel Mortemart. On her arrival, taking a key from her pocket, she opened a little wicket-door, and taking my hand, led me to the second-floor, and knocked in a peculiar manner. A man apparently of about forty-eight or fifty years of age opened the door. He was dressed like a working man, and had all the appearances of being engaged as a bookbinder: But, in the first words he uttered—his expression of thanks —the well-bred nobleman was apparent.

"Sir," said he to me, "Providence has sent you to me, and it is as an envoy of Providence that I receive you. Is it true that you can save me—and, above all, that you wish to save me?"

I told him the whole affair, and that Marceau had authorised me to bring him in the capacity of his secretary, asking nothing but a promise that he would not carry arms against his country.

"Gladly I make this promise to you," he exclaimed, "and to the General I will renew it. But when does Marceau depart?"

"To-morrow."

"Ought I to go to him to-night?"

"Whenever you please: he awaits you."

The father and daughter looked at each other inquiringly.

"My father, I think it would be more prudent for you to go to the general to-night," said Solange.

"Where does Marceau reside?"

"Rue de la Université, No. 40, at the house of his sister, Mdlle. Desgraviers-Marceau."

"Will you accompany us?"

"I will follow at a short distance, and will bring back mademoiselle after you have entered the house."

"But how will Marceau know me to be the party of whom you have spoken to him?"

"You must give him this tricolor cockade—it is the sign of recognition."

"And what can I do for my liberator?"

"You will confide to me the safety of your daughter, as she has confided yours to me."

"Agreed."

So saying, he took his hat, and extinguishing the light, led the way to the stairs. At the door, he took his daughter's arm, and, by the way of the rue Saint Pères, gained the rue de l'Université, whilst I followed at about ten paces behind.—We met no one on our road: I rejoined them at the door.

"This is a good omen," said I. "Now, do you wish me to wait here, or shall I go up stairs with you?"

"No—I will not further compromise you— wait till my daughter comes out."

I bowed.

"Once more, thanks and farewell," said he to me, holding out his hand. "Words cannot express the sentiments with which your genero-

sity has inspired me. I trust that God will one day put me in a position to show my gratitude to you."

My only response was a warm pressure of his hand. He entered the house, followed by Solange, who also shook my hand warmly at parting: After waiting about ten minutes, the door was opened, and Solange again made her appearance.

"All is well?" inquired I.

"All well," she answered: "your friend is indeed worthy of the name; for he has treated us with the greatest delicacy. Surmising that I should be happy to remain with my dear father till the moment of his departure, his sister has made up a bed for me in her chamber. At three o'clock to-morrow, my father will be safe. If you think the thanks of a daughter who owes to you her fathers' life are worth the trouble of listening to, you will look for me in the rue Féron at this hour to-morrow."

"Rest assured I shall be there. Has your father nothing to say to me?"

"He begged me to ask you to send me to him as soon as possible."

"That shall be whenever you wish it, Solange," said I, with an aching heart.

"It will be necessary, at least, that I first learn where to rejoin my father," said she. "Oh! you have not got rid of me yet."

I took her hand and pressed it to my heart. She presented her brow to me as of old. "To-morrow!" said she. Pressing my lips to her forehead, I pressed not only her hand, but her glowing, trembling bosom—her bounding, fluttering heart—to mine.

It was with a light heart and a joyous soul that I entered my home. My heart was light with the proud consciousness of having done a good action; my soul was in a tumult of joy because I had gained the love of this charming creature. I know not now whether on that night I slept or whether I was awake. I only know that to me it seemed as if all the harmony of nature was pouring forth its glad song into my soul; the night appeared to me as one blissful, interminable period—the day vast, illimitable, and redolent of happiness. I felt, though anxious that the time should pass quickly that I might again see Solange, yet as if I wished to retard it, fearing to lose a moment of the happy hours that flew over my existence. At nine o'clock the next day, I was waiting in the Rue Feron. At half-past nine, Solange made her appearance. She came to me, and throwing her arms around my neck, exclaimed: "Saved! my father is saved, and to you does he owe his liberty, his life. Oh, I love you!"

Five days after after this, Solange received a letter, announcing her father's safe arrival in England. The next day I had procured a passport and carried it to Solange. On taking it from me, she burst into tears.

"You do not then love me?" said she.

"I love you better than my life," I replied, "but I have given my word of honour to your father, and, before all things—before life or love —I must keep my word."

"Then," said she, "it is I who must break

mine. If thou hast the courage, dear Albert, to let me depart from thee, I—I have not the courage to quit thy side."

Alas! she remained.

___

CHAPTER VII.

ALBERT.

As, in the first interruption of M. Ledru's narrative, so at the present moment, there was a temporary silence—a silence more profound, more respectful than the first, for we felt that we were approaching the catastrophe of the history; and M. Ledru had intimated that he might not probably have strength of nerve to conclude it. But after a short pause he proceeded.

"Three months had quickly sped away since the night when I had put the question of departure to Solange: and, during that time, not a syllable was broached by either of us on the subject. Solange had wished to reside in the Rue Taranne. I had taken one for her under the name of Solange—I had never known her by any other—never had she known me but as Albert. I had procured her a situation as under-governess in a boarding-school for young ladies, in order the more surely to secure her from the prying researches of the revolutionary police, now become more active than ever. Sundays and Tuesdays we passed in each other's company in our little apartment in the Rue Taranne: from our bed-room we could see the spot where we had first encountered each other. Every day we received a letter: hers was addressed to Solange, mine was to Albert.

"Those three months were the happiest of my life."

"In the meantime, I had not renounced the design which I had determined in my own mind after the conversation I had had with the headsman's assistant. I had asked for and obtained permission to experimentize on the assumed persistence of life after the infliction of capital punishment; and these experiments all tended to strengthen if not demonstrate the fact that agony—and that the most intense—survived the actual blow."

"Ah! that is the very thing I deny." said the doctor.

"Look you," said M. Ledru, "you surely will not deny that the knife strikes the condemned in a part of the body the most sensitive, because that at that point the nerves are all combined and gathered into a small compass? Nor will you deny that within the small compass of the neck are enclosed the leading nerves of the human system—the sympathetic, the erratic, the phrenetic, and the spinal marrow itself, the source of the nerves which serve the inferior members? Can you deny that the breaking—the crashing of this vertebral column—does not produce the most awful and intense suffering the human system can experience?"

"Granted," said the doctor, "but this suffering is but of a few second's duration."

"Oh! that, in my turn, I distinctly deny," said M. Ledru, with the earnest expression of conviction in his tone, "but if this intense agony endures only for a few seconds, during these few seconds, the feeling, the individuality, the mind, the man himself, is alive; the head hears, sees, feels, and judges of its separation from its body, and who shall say that the short duration of this suffering can atone for its horrible intensity.*

"So, in your opinion, the Decree of the Constituent Assembly, which substituted the guillotine for all other capital punishments, was a great philanthropic error, and it would have been much more humane to hang than decapitate?"

"It is an indisputable fact, that many who have hanged themselves, or have been hanged, have been resuscitated. Very well: those who have thus recovered have testified as to the sensation they have undergone. It is the same as that felt in an apopletic stroke: that is, a deep and profound sleep, during which no particular or acute pain is felt—no agonising sensation whatever—but preceded by a sort of flashing of brilliant lights across the eyes, which, little by little, changes into a dull dense blue, then into utter and thick darkness—after that, the sufferer falls into a state of syncope. And, in fact, doctor, you know this to be the truth as well as any one. In the case of a man who has lost a portion of the cranium, so as to lay bare the surface of the brain, press a finger upon the spot, that man experiences no acute perception of pain; he is only insensible or comatose. Exactly the same phenomenon takes place when the brain is compressed by a sudden rush or accession of blood; and equally so in the case of a man hung, the blood is accumulated and pressed on to the brain: because, in the first place, the blood, entering the brain by the vertebral arteries, which, traversing as they do the boney canals of the neck, are secured from the effect of compression, whilst, at the same time, this accumulated arterial blood is prevented from returning to the body, owing to the closing of the return canals by the pressure of the cord upon the veins."

"Very true," said the doctor, "but let us return to the experimental part of the story. I am very anxious to hear about this famous talking head."

I fancied I heard something very like a sigh escape from M. Ledru. Owing to the darkness, it was not possible to catch a glimpse of his features.

"Yes," said he, "I have started from my subject, doctor, I will resume! Unhappily, there is no fear of my forgetting the facts.

"The executions at this period were more numerous than ever: thirty or forty unhappy criminals were guillotined every day; and so great was the torrent of blood shed in the Place de la Revolution, that they been obliged to make a trench of three feet in depth around the scaffold, and cover the ditch with planks. On one of these sanguinary occasions, one of the

* It is not with a view to satisfy a morbid love of the horrible that we dwell on such a painful subject, but it appears to us that, at a moment when the expediency of abolishing capital punishment is often the subject of discussion, the few remarks here ventured may not be without their utility.

The pseudo-bookbinder.

frail coverings gave way under a lad of eight or nine years of age : he fell into this sea of blood, and was drowned or rather suffocated.

"I should here state that I took especial care not to let Solange have any knowledge of the peculiar occupation in which I passed those hours when absent from her; indeed, at the first outset I had great difficulty not only in overcoming my repugnance to handling, examining and experimenting on these poor remains of humanity, but still more so from a feeling that I might possibly be adding to their tortures. I finally satisfied my scruples by reflecting that those experiments were as necessary to the development of facts as my studies; that I was only anxious to obtain a knowledge which would have for its object the benefit of the human race ; and that if at some future time legislators should adopt my convictions, I might be happily the instrument of totally abolishing capital punishment throughout civilized countries.

"As fast as my researches gave results, I committed them to writing. At about the end of two months, I had pretty nearly gone through all the various experiments which my own reflection or the suggestions of others could afford me. Still I resolved to push my researches as far as possible ; and for that purpose I had recourse to the aid of galvanism and electricity. I had obtained free access to the Cemetery of Clamart : and the bodies of all those who were condemned were placed at my

SOTAIN.

"The dreadful cry still rings in my ears."—*Page* 39

disposal. They also constructed for me a laboratory, or rather changed a little chapel built in one corner of the cemetery into an arena for my researches. You know that, having hunted their kings from the throne, the revolutionary fanatics finished by trying to thrust the Deity from the churches. Well— in this place I had set up my electrical apparatus, and three or four of those galvanic instruments then called ' *excitateurs*.' At five o'clock each day the horrible cargo arrived; the bodies piled pell-mell in the tumbril, the heads thrown pell-mell into a sack. I took, hap-hazard, one or two of the heads and bodies, the rest were thrown indiscriminately into the common grave. The heads which had been subjected to the experiments were added to the next day's convoy. On most occasions my brother assisted me in my researches.

In the midst of this daily contact with the dead, my love for Solange increased hourly: whilst, on her side, that love was reciprocated with all the intensity of a devoted woman. Oftentimes I had thought to make her my wife ; oftentimes we had talked over the happiness of such an union ; but to become my wife, it would be necessary for her to reveal her name, and the revelation of that name—the name of an emigrant, of an aristocrat, of a prescribed family, would have carried with it instant death. Her father had written to her many times, to hasten her departure from France : but she had told him of our love for each other, and had asked his consent to our union, which he had given. So far, all was well. In the meantime, in the midst of all the terrible events of the period, an event more horrible than any occurred to afflict us. It was the trial of Marie Antoinette. Commencing on the 4th of October, the trial was followed up with energy : on the 14th she was brought before the revolutionary tribunal ; on the 16th, at four o'clock in the morning she was condemned ; at one o'clock on the same day she mounted the scaffold. That morning I received a note from Solange, informing me that she did not like to pass such a day without seeing me. At about two o'clock I reached our little apartment in the Rue Taranne ; I found Solange in tears. I myself was deeply affected with this execution : the queen had shown me so many kindnesses in my youth, that their remembrance had sank deep in my heart. Ah ! I shall ever remember that day—it was a Wednesday. There was something in Paris on that day more than sorrow—it was horror. For myself I experienced a strange heaviness of heart—a strong foreboding of some approaching and terrible calamity. I exerted myself to raise the spirits of Solange, who had thrown herself weeping into my arms,—but the words of consolation would not flow from my lips because its source was dried up in my own heart. We passed, as usual, the night together ; the night was more depressive than the day. I was aroused from my first sleep by the howling of a dog shut up in the apartment below ours—and this was continued until past two o'clock in the morning. The cause of this unusual disturbance we ascertained next day : the owner of the dog had gone out, after locking the door ; he had been arrested in the street, conducted to the revolutionary tribunal, condemned at three o'clock in the morning—executed at four.

It was now necessary that we should separate, Solange's classes would be assembled at nine o'clock, the boarding-school she attended was situated near the Jardin des Plantes. I hesitated a long time before I could consent to her departure ; of herself she was unable to command resolution enough to leave me. But to have remained two days without visiting the school might have led to enquiry—a thing very dangerous to persons circumstanced like Solange. I called a *voiture*, and went with her as far as the corner of the Rue des Fossés-Saint-Bernard. Whilst on the road, we lay locked in each other's arms—not a word was spoken by either of us, but our tears ran down our cheeks to our lips, mingling the bitterness of grief with the sweet kisses of affection. I descended from the fiacre, but, in place of going by its side, I remained motionless, my eyes fixed upon the vehicle which held all I loved. After running fifty yards, the vehicle suddenly stopped ; Solange put her head out at the window, as if she had known that I should remain gazing after her. I ran to her, ascended the fiacre, shut the window, and again pressed her to my heart. At this moment, the hour of nine sounded forth from the church of St. Stephen-on-the-Mount. Drying my tears, imprinting a triple kiss on her lips, I jumped to the ground, and ran from the spot.

I fancied I heard Solange calling me back to her, but I was afraid that those tears, those hesitations, might be remarked by passers-by. I had the fatal courage to persist in my flight ; I entered my room in a state bordering on distraction. The day I passed in writing to Solange, in the evening I sent my volume of a letter to her ; I had just returned from posting my letter when I received one from herself. It informed me that she had been severely censured, had been asked a multitude of questions, and they had threatened to take from her her next holiday. This would have been on the following Sunday, but Solange solemnly swore to me in her note that whether she broke with the mistress of the boarding-house or not, on that day she would see me whatever might happen. I added my oath to hers, for it seemed to me that if I were not to see her for seven days, which would inevitably be the case if they deprived her of her first day out, I should have gone mad. Besides these disagreeables, Solange had informed me of a graver source of disquietude : a letter sent to her by her father had been left at the boarding school : when she received it, it bore evident traces of the seal having been broken. I passed a miserable night—and a worse day on the morrow. I had written, as usual, to Solange, and, as it was my experimental day, about three o'clock I went to my brother's home, in order to bring him with me to Clamart : but as he was from home, I went alone. The weather was horrible : the bare earth was saturated with rain—that cold, torrent like rain which is the herald of winter. All along the road I could hear the harsh and vulgar tones of itinerants howling out a list of the condemned of the day : it was numerous—and comprised men, women, and children. The harvest of blood was an abundant one ; and there was no lack of subjects for my anatomical experiments of the night. Night set in very early : at four o'clock indeed, at which hour I reached Clamart, it was nearly dark. The dreary aspect of the cemetery, with its vast arena of newly raised mounds, and its few dark and skeleton-looking trees swaying and rattling their bare branches to and fro in the wind, formed a picture at once dismal and hideous. Where the ground was not upturned it was covered by burnt-up-grass or nettles : but each day saw those miserable patches of rank verdure invaded by fresh interments. In the midst of these uprisings of the soil, the common grave of the day gaped widely for its prey : they had anticipated the increase in the list of condemned, and the deep yawning chasm was of greater extent than usual. I approached the ditch mechanically : the bottom was covered with water. As I gazed into the dark and flooded ditch, destined for the reception of the cold and naked victims of the morrow, my feet slipped over the edge, and I was precipitated into the grave : my hair stood on end with affright. Wet through, my teeth chattering with cold, I scrambled out and repaired to my laboratory. This had been, as I have before told you, an ancient chapel attached to the cemetery. I looked around—what was I seeking ? I cannot tell. I cast my eyes around till they rested on the wall, at a spot where formerly had stood an altar : the wall was bare

—the altar was rased. In the spot where formerly had been the tabernacle—that is to say, the emblem of God—of life, they had placed a fleshless, hairless skull—the emblem of death—of annihilation. I lighted my candle: placed myself at my table, which was covered with utensils and instruments of strange form, and which I had invented myself; I sat down, and was soon plunged in thought. Of what did I think? of the poor queen whom I had in my youth seen so fair, so happy, so much beloved: who, but yesterday, followed by the imprecations of the mob, had been drawn in a cart to the scaffold; and who, at that moment slept, a headless corpse, in a common grave—she who erst had pillowed her head under the gilded ceilings of the Tuilleries, Versailles, and St. Cloud. Whilst thus plunged in the depth of my gloomy reflections the rain fell in torrents, the wind, in long gusty squalls, wailed mournfully through the leafless branches of the trees and the long rank reedy grass of the cemetery. With this lugubrious chaunt came ever and anon as it were the deep bass of thunder—which seemed not to proceed from the sky but to roll over the earth—which trembled with its reverberations. It was not thunder—it was the harsh rumbling wheels of the revolutionary cart, with its usual load of headless trunks and trunkless heads; it had left the Place de la Revolution and was now entering the cemetery at Clamart. The chapel door was opened, and two men entered, bearing between them a sack. One of them was the same Légros that I had visited whilst in prison; the other was a gravedigger.

"See, Monsieur Ledru," said the executioner's assistant to me, "what a lot we have brought you! We shall not hurry you to night, but shall leave you the whole batch and bury them to-morrow, when we shall have daylight; there is no fear of their catching the rheumatism by passing a night in the open air." So saying, with a brutal grin, the two purveyors to Death placed the sack in the corner of the wall, near the ancient altar of the chapel, and went out without shutting the door after them, letting in the gusts of cold air, which made my candle flicker and flare with a sickly pale flame around the long black wick. I heard them detach the horse, shut the cemetery gate, and depart, leaving behind them the tumbril full of bodies. I had a great wish to have gone at the same moment: still I know not what power kept me, all cold and shivering as I was, in the place. Certainly it was not fear: but the rush of the fitful wind, the beating and plashing of the rain, the mournful soughing of the trees as they were twisted and contorted as 'twere in agony, the trembling, uncertain light, disturbed as it was by the wind, all fell on me with a vague sensation of terror. Suddenly, it appeared to me that I heard a voice, sweet though mournful in its tones—a voice which seemed to proceed from the altar piece, and which pronounced the name "Albert." At that word I started, wild with terror, for there was but one being who knew me by that name. I turned my eyes slowly round the little chapel, which, small as it was, was but scantily lighted, and involuntarily fixed them on the sack resting under the altar, and of which the bloody and

bulged appearance told plainly of its horrible contents, when I again heard the same plaintive voice, but in a still more mournful strain, repeating the same name:—

"Albert!"

I felt petrified with affright; the voice seemed to come from the interior of the sack. I was now in that state of mind when the extremity of terror gives a man courage to dare all. Slowly and deliberately I walked to the sack, and, plunging my hand into it, I took out the first head which I grasped, and regaining my chair, into which I fell rather than sat, I placed it on the table before me.

Oh! that dreadful cry which burst from me still rings in my ears. That head, the lips of which were yet moist and warm, its eyes half shut, was the head of Solange. I was maddened—three times I cried out:—

"Solange! Solange! Solange!"

At the third cry, the eyes reopened and looked at me whilst a tear from each eye slowly traced their way down the cheeks, threw a burning glance of love on me—as if it was the last effort of the departing soul to express its never dying passion—and closed for ever.

I arose maddened—insensate—furious; I wished to fly. In rising, my coat caught the table, overthrew it, and with it the candle, which was extinguished, whilst the head rolled along the floor to where I stood. I fell to the ground, and it seemed to me as if the head, rolling along the flags of the chapel, pressed its lips to my own; a freezing coldness ran through my very bones—I uttered a groan and fainted.

At six o'clock the morning after, the gravedigger found me cold and senseless as the stones on which I was stretched.

Solange, recognised by the lost letter of her father's, had been arrested, condemned, and executed, all in one day. That head which spoke to me, those eyes which threw their lurid gaze on mine, those lips which had pressed mine, even in death, were the head, the eyes, the lips of Solange.

"You know, Lenoir," said M. Ledru, turning towards the chevalier, "at that time I was at the brink of death."

CHAPTER IV.

THE effect produced by the recital of M. Ledru was overpowering. None dreamt of offering any observations; even the doctor was silent. The Chevalier Lenoir, called upon to testify to the fact by M. Ledru, responded by a simple nod of acquiescence; the pale lady, who had for an instant risen upright on the sofa, had again fallen back into the depth of its cushions, and gave no signs of life except by an occasional sigh; the commissary of police, seeing nothing in the story to make an authorised minute of, forgot to whisper even a word. For myself, I mentally took notes of all the details, in order to relate them at some future time: and as to Alliette and the Abbé Moulle, the adventure tallied too completely with their ideas to furnish a handle for objection. On the

ED. COPPIN

Turning round——I saw &c.—*Page* 42.

contrary, the Abbé Moule was the first to break silence, and take up in some sort the general opinion:

"I sincerely believe that which you have recounted, my dear Ledru: but how do you explain this *fact*—as we say in common place talk?"

"I do not seek to explain anything:" answered M. Ledru: "I have narrated it—and that is all I shall attempt."

"Yes—how do you explain *that*?" said the doctor: "for, whatever may be your opinion respecting the tenacity of life, you will not admit that at the expiration of two hours, a human head, severed from the trunk, can talk, see, and act?"

"If I could have accounted for it, my dear doctor, I should not have had, as its immediate consequence, that dangerous fit of illness."

"But, doctor," said the Chevalier Lenoir, "how do you account for it? for of course you are not prepared to think that Ledru has invented this story for his own pleasure: his sickness, at all events, was a material and undoubted fact."

"Parbleu! it's a very simple affair. Hallucination was the cause. M. Ledru believed he saw—M. Ledru believed he heard; it was exactly to his mind as if he had seen and heard. The organs which transmit perception to the sensorium—that is to say, the brain,—had been disordered by circumstances exciting an undue influence on them. They were disordered—and being so disordered, transmitted false impressions; in such instances, to believe to have seen is to see: believe you hear, and you do hear. The cold, the rain, the darkness, had disordered M. Ledru's sentient organs—hence what followed. Thus madmen infallibly, as far as

"There was no more a cat in the room than there is in my arms."—*Page 42.*

impressions are concerned, hear and see whatever their disordered organs convey to the brain : the illusion itself may be merely momentary—the remembrance of the illusion remains after the illusion is past. There is the whole affair explained at once."

"But how when the illusion never disappears?" asked the Abbé Moulle.

"Very well : then the disease comes under the category of incurable, and the patient dies."

"Have you ever attended persons afflicted with this species of disease, doctor ?"

"No ; but I know many medical men who have, and, among others, a celebrated doctor who accompanied Sir Walter Scott on his voyage to France."

"Did he give you any information ?"

"He told me a story somewhat similar to that related by our host—but perhaps even more singular."

"And can you explain that also by reference to natural causes ?" asked the Abbé Moulle.

"Assuredly."

"And this story, narrated to you by the English physician, will you let us hear it ?"

"Doubtless."

"The story ! the story ! go on."

"Must I ?"

"Not a doubt of it," was the universal answer.

"So be it. The physician who attended Sir Walter Scott was called Simpson, one of the most distinguished members of the faculty in Edinburgh, he was consequently on terms of intimacy with many of the highest families in that city. Among these was a judge of one of the criminal courts—whose name I don't know, for that was the only thing kept secret in the affair. This judge, who was attended by the doctor in his capacity of medical man of the family, seemed, without being affected by any apparent derangement of health, to be wasting away, a deep melancholy appeared to have settled on him. The members of his family had on several occasions questioned the doctor, and the doctor had as often interrogated his friend as to the cause of this, but had received only vague responses,—which only served to strengthen their fears by proving that some secret was hidden from them which the patient was determined not to make known. At last, the doctor so urgently insisted on his friend divulging the nature of the malady which so depressed him and afflicted his friends, that taking the doctor by the hand, with a sorrowful smile he said to the physician :

"Yes—yes—I am ill, and my illness, my dear doctor, so much the more difficult to cure, because it exists only in my own imagination."

"How—in your imagination ?"

"Yes : I am becoming insane."

"Insane! in what way, I beg to ask you ? You have a clear eye, a calm voice, and," here he felt his pulse, " a regular pulsation."

"And in these facts you see exactly the features which make my case more serious : it is a malady, the progress of which I can perceive and judge of."

"But in what way does your madness evince itself ?"

"Shut the door, to avoid interruption, and I will tell you all about it."

The Doctor shut the door, and took a chair by his friend's side.

"You recollect," said the judge, "the last trial for a capital offence in which I was called on to pronounce death ?"

"Yes, it was the case of a Scotchman, whom you sentenced to be hung for burglary, and who met his fate accordingly."

"Exaclty. Well, at the moment after I had sentenced him, he made a gesture of menace towards me, whilst flames seemed to flash forth from his eyes. I did not pay much attention to this circumstance, for such threats are common on the part of the condemned. But on the morning after the execution, the hangman came to my house, and, humbly begging pardon for his presumption, declared that he felt it his duty to communicate to me a fact he had learnt in connection with the defunct criminal : it was that he had died pronouncing some mystical conjuration against me, averring that to-morrow at six o'clock—this was the hour fixed for his execution—I should see some very strange thing. I had some idea that the criminal intended me some act of revenge from the hands of his companions, so, at six o'clock, I shut myself up in my study, with a pair of loaded pistols on my desk. My mind had been pre-occupied all the day with this revelation of the hangman, and I confess it was with some anxiety I heard the timepiece strike the hour of six. As the last stroke of the hammer vibrated upon the bell, I heard a sort of purring, of which I was ignorant as to the cause. Turning round to see from what the noise emanated, I saw a large tortoise-shell cat. How it came there it was impossible to tell ; the doors and windows were close shut ; it must have been accidentally shut up in the room during the day. Having no particular taste for the company of my feline visitor, I rang the bell for my servant ; the door being fastened from within, I had to rise to let him in. On his entry I spoke to him of the tortoiseshell cat being in the room. However, we could see no traces of it, though we searched very carefully all parts of the room. I thought no more of the affair. But the next evening, as I was sitting alone, I again heard the same purring noise as I had done the day before, and, turning round I saw the same cat. As soon as I saw him, he jumped from the floor on to my knees. I have no antipathy to cats, yet I must say the animal's familiarity caused a disagreeable sensation. I drove him from his position : but he was no sooner on the ground than again he sprang on me. A second attempt produced the same result. At a last resource, I rose, and walked about the room : the cat followed me, step by step : annoyed at this persistence, I rang the bell : my servant entered. But the cat ran under the bed : in vain we tried to discover and dislodge it,—once under the bed we could see no more of it. I went out the next day to visit two or three friends : then I returned to my house, into which I let myself by a latch-key. As I had no light, I went slowly and softly up the staircase, for fear of treading on something. On reaching the last step, I heard my servant talking to my wife's chambermaid. My own name being pronounced, drew my attention to this conversation ; and then I discovered that it was a recital of the adventures with the cat on the two days preceding—only with this addition. "Master must be losing his wits— these was no more a tortoiseshell cat in the room than there is now in my hands."

These words frightened me. Either what I saw was a reality or an illusion : if real, I was the subject of a supernatural visitation ; if false —if I believed I saw a thing which had no existence—then I must be losing my senses.

You can surmise, my dear friend, with what impatience, not unmixed with fear, I looked forward to the hour of six. The next day, under pretence of re-arranging my room, I keep my man near me : he was in the room standing by my side when the clock struck six—and at the same moment I heard the purring noise, and saw my tormentor, the eternal cat, complacently sitting by my side. I remained silent for a few moments, hoping that my servant would catch sight of the animal and speak of it first ; but he passed to and fro in the room without giving a sign of seeing such a thing. I seized the opportunity, when my man was in such a position that to come towards me he would inevitably have had to walk over the cat, to call him to me.

"Bring the handbell to my table, John," said I.

He was standing at the head of my bed ; the handbell was on the mantle-piece : in order to go from the bed's head to the fireplace it was absolutely impossible not to walk over the spot where the cat sat. He walked on; but at the moment when his next footstep must have been on the animal, it jumped from the floor to my knees.

John did not see it, or, at all events, did not appear to see it.

I confess to you that I felt a cold perspiration standing on my brow, and that the words, "Master must be losing his wits," had in my mind a terrible significancy.

"John," said I to him, "do you see anything on my knees?"

John looked hard at me. Then, like a man taking a sudden resolve, he answered: Yes, sir, I see a cat."

What a load was taken off my mind! I breathed freely once more. I took the cat, and said to him: "In that case, John, carry it out-side, I beg of you."

He put his hands under mine, and putting the animal under his arm, he went out with it.

Though somewhat reassured, I looked around me for some minutes in a state of great anxiety, but, not perceiving anything of the animal, I resolved to see what John had done with it. I had left my chamber with the inten-tion of asking him, when, on putting my foot on the step of the saloon, I heard a great noise of laughter which issued from my wife's dressing-room. Approaching very softly on tip-toe, I heard John say to the chambermaid:

"I tell you, Mary, master is getting quite silly. He believes, you know, that he is con-tinually seeing a tortoiseshell cat; to-night, he asked me if I did not see a cat on his knees."

"And what answer did you give him?" asked the girl.

"By jingo! I told him I did see it," said John. "Poor man! I would not wish to contradict him. Guess, now, what I did."

"How can I guess such a thing?"

"Well, I'll tell you. I pretended to take the cat from his knees, and clap it under my arm. Then he said to me, 'Take it away!—take it away!' I made as if I went out with it, and he was quite pleased."

"But how could you carry the cat away when there was no cat."

"No—no; I tell you the cat only existed in his fancy. Now, what good should I have done if I had told him the truth? he would, perhaps, have given me my discharge. If he likes to give me five-and-twenty pounds a-year to see a cat, I shall of course do so—aye, thirty cats, if he wishes it."

I had not moral courage sufficient to enable me to hear more. I sighed, and went back to my room.

On the morrow, at six o'clock, I found my companion the cat at his old place. Will you believe it, my friend, continued the unhappy man, that, for one month, the same apparition was renewed every evening; in fact, I was becoming habituated to its presence, when, on the thirtieth day after the execution, six o'clock struck, and the cat had failed in its visit. I flattered myself that I had got rid of my tor-mentor, and I could scarcely sleep for joy. The

next day, the time crept, so to speak, so anxious was I to arrive at the fated hour. From five to six, my eyes never quitted the timepiece, but followed the hand as it moved, second by second. At last it reached the numerals XII.—I.—II. —III.—IV.—V.—and VI. at last. As the sixth stroke fell vibrating on my ear, the door opened, said the unhappy magistrate, and I saw enter an usher, dressed in the livery of the household of a lord chamberlain of the court. My first idea was that some officer of the house-hold had sent for me, and I almost instinctively held out my hand for the note: the usher took not the least notice of my gesture, but placed himself behind my easy chair. I had no need to turn myself round to face my strange visitor, for a mirror hung opposite, and by it I had a full view of him. I rose and walked about, he fol-lowed me a few paces distant; I came back to the table and rang the bell, the servant ap-peared, but the presence of the usher seemed as much a myth to him as was that of the cat. I therefore sent him back, and remained alone with my gentleman usher—whom I had full leisure to contemplate and examine at my ease. He was dressed in court livery, wore a bag-wig and embroidered vest, carried a sword at his side, and his hat under his arm. At ten o'clock, I retired to rest: my visitor, as if wishing to pass the night as comfortably as possible, sat himself in my easy chair, exactly opposite my bed. I turned my face to the wall: but as I was restless, and sleep was out of the question, I frequently turned—whenever I did so, I saw by the light of the night lamp, the usher still seated in the chair opposite. At length, I saw the grey light of the moon stealing into my chamber through the openings of the blinds; I turned a last look towards the chair: it was empty—the usher had disappeared; and until night I saw him no more. That night there was a grand reception at Lord B——'s house; under pretence of arranging my toilette, I called my servant at five minutes before six o'clock, ordering him to bolt the door on the inside, which he did. As the clock struck six, I fixed my eyes on the door: it opened, and my attendant usher entered. I went immediately to the door: the bolt was fastened; and the bolt bore no trace of having left its hold. I turned—the usher was behind my chair, and John went about his work in the room without betraying a thought of any one's presence beside my own. It was plain to me, therefore, that John saw no more of the man than he had of the animal. I proceeded to dress: and now appeared to my astonished eyes a most singular circumstance. Assiduous in his attention, my new comrade assisted John in everything he did, and without John ever having the slightest notion of the help so freely given. So, if John held my coat by the collar, the phantom usher held it by the lappels; and whilst John pre-sented me my small clothes by the waistband, the usher held the legs. I had never seen a domestic so extremely officious.

The time for my departure arrived. Then, instead of following me, the usher preceded me, gliding through the door of my chamber, de-scending the stairs, his hat under his arm, behind

The phantom Usher.

John, who opened the door of the carriage, and, when John had shut it and taken his place in the dickey behind, he jumped upon the front, and seated himself on the left of the coachman. The coach stopped at Lord B——'s door; John opened the door, but the phantom was at his post immediately behind him. Scarcely had I put foot to ground when the usher flew before him, passing through the crowd of domestics which encumbered the entrance, and looking behind to see if I followed. It struck me at that moment that I would essay upon the coachman the same proof I had sought from my servant.

"Patrick," said I to the coachman, "who was that man with you?"

"What man, sir?" said the coachman.

"The man who sat on the box with you whilst coming here."

Patrick turned his great eyes round in perfect astonishment.

"No matter," said I, "I mistook." So saying, I entered the mansion. My phantom attendant had ascended the stairs, and awaited me on the landing. When I reached the top, he again preceded me, as if for the purpose of announcing my arrival: this done, he withdrew into the antechamber, among the domestics in waiting: but here also his presence was unknown—he was invisible to all excepting myself.

From that moment my fear changed to terror: and I saw plainly that my intellect was failing

The Skeleton.

me: it was on that occasion that the change you and others have perceived was first apparent: I was asked—and amongst others by yourself, doctor—as to the cause of my absence and taciturnity.

In the antechamber I was again in company with my courteous tormentor: again he mounted the box seat, again preceded me into my room, and again took up his station at the back of my chair.

Then came the wish to learn if there was any thing real or tangible in this phantom usher.— I reached out over the back of my chair. I felt nothing: still I could see the smirking obsequious countenance of my infernal tormentor. Again, on retiring to rest, was I doomed to see him seat himself in my *fauteuil*.

In short, this daily torment lasted a whole month: at the end of which I was released from its influence for one day. But no joyful anticipations of having outlived my torment gladdened my heart on this occasion; on the contrary, I awaited in dread anxiety some more terrible modification of the phantasy which was eating my soul: I shuddered at the thoughts of what to-morrow's dreaded hour would bring forth. It came: as the hour struck, I heard a slight rustling of my bed curtains; looking up, I saw, betwixt the curtains, which it held half open, a human skeleton. There it stood immoveable, its void eyes staring—if I might use the term—at me: I rose—I walked about the room: but wherever I went, still the death's head grinned and leered at me—following my every evolution. Bereft of all courage, I no longer sought my couch, but rested myself, my eyes shut, in the chair. In the morning, I was freed for the remainder of the day from this ghastly apparition. I ordered my servant to change the position of my bed, and to cross the curtains. But all was useless: at six came the same rustling noise, the curtains were separated by the bony hands of the grim spectre, and the skeleton took its old place betwixt the curtains of my bed.

Wearied out with watching and anxiety, I resolved to go to my bed. Horror! as I lay down, the hideous skeleton seemed to incline its visage towards me—its eyeless orbits seemed to peer into my eyes with a horrible leer—a frightful mockery of glee.

"Now, doctor, you may guess what a night I passed! I tell you I have passed nine such nights. Now you know why I am depressed—why I am steeped in melancholy thought—why I am wasting, body and mind—will you undertake to cure me?"

"At least I will try," answered the doctor.

"How will you do it?"

"I am convinced that this phantasy has only its existence in your diseased imagination."

"What matters it whether it has an existence or not, if I must see it?"

"Would you wish that I try if I can see it as well as yourself?"

"I should wish nothing better."

"When shall we begin?"

"The sooner the better; say to-morrow."

"To-morrow let it be. Until then keep up your spirits."

The unhappy patient replied by a sickly smile. The next day, at seven in the morning, the doctor repaired to the chamber of his friend.

"Well, my dear friend, where's the skeleton?" asked the doctor.

"It has just disappeared," replied the patient in a feeble voice.

"Well—well—we will so arrange matters that he shall not appear to-night at any rate."

"Do it."

"In the first place, you tell me that this phantom infallibly makes its appearance as the clock strikes six?"

"To a second."

"We will begin, then, by stopping the timepiece:" so saying, he stopped the vibration of the pendulum.

"Why do you stop the clock?"

"I wish you to lose the power of measuring time."

"Good."

"With the same view we will close the window shutters, and pull down the blinds."—This was done and candles were brought and lighted.

"Now, John," said the doctor to my domestic: "keep luncheon and dinner ready for us, but do not send it up at the usual hour, but only when I call for it. Now, bring cards, dice, and dominoes, and leave the room."

This was done, and the doctor and his patient were left to themselves. The doctor commenced by engaging the attention of the sick man, now talking to him, now playing a game at cards, then throwing the dice. After some time, feeling hungry, he rang the bell for luncheon. This was brought. After luncheon, play was recommenced; only to be interrupted by the doctor ringing for dinner to be served. They ate, they drank; took their coffee after dinner; and again had recourse to the various devices the doctor had contrived to while the time away: The day appeared to each of them intolerably long, thus closeted alone: but the doctor confidently believed that he had measured the time very nearly in his own mind, and was convinced that the fatal hour had long since passed.

"Bravo!" said he, rising from his seat, "victory! victory!"

"How—victory!—what mean you?" asked the sick man.

"I mean that it is now eight or nine o'clock, at the least, and you have missed your evening visitor."

"Look at your watch, my dear doctor, since it is the only indication of time in the house; and on my word, if it is past the hour, I shall gladly join in your exultation, and cry 'Victory!' as loud."

The doctor took out his watch, looked at it, but spoke not a word.

"You are mistaken, are you not, doctor?" said the patient, "it is now exactly six o'clock."

"Well—what of that?"

"What of it?—look there—the skeleton has just made its appearance."

The doctor looked round the room.

"Where do you see it?" asked he.

"In its usual place—betwixt my bed curtains."

The doctor rose from his seat, and stood in the opening of the bed-curtains, in the place indicated by the sick man.

"Now," said he, "can you see the skeleton?"

"I see nothing of its body, which is hidden by yours, but I can see its skull."

"Where?"

"Just above your right shoulder. It is just as if you had two heads—one living, the other dead."

In spite of himself, the doctor shuddered and turned round, but he could see nothing.

"My dear friend," said he, to the sick man, in a tone of pity, "if you have any disposition to make with regard to your property, you had better do it at once."

So saying, he took his leave. Nine days afterwards, John, on entering his master's chamber, found him lying dead in his bed.

It was three months to a day after the execution of the burglar.

CHAPTER IX.

MYSTERY V.—THE SEPULCHRE OF SAINT DENIS.

"VERY good," said M. Ledru, as the doctor ended the narrative. "What does that prove, doctor?"

"It proves this, that the organs which are employed in the transmission of perception to the brain are liable, in certain cases and under a peculiar train of circumstances, to become deranged, and, like an unfaithful mirror, transmit distorted or wrong impressions to the mind? in such cases objects are seen and sounds heard which have no real body or existence."

"However," said the chevalier Lenoir, with the diffidence of a truly learned man, "however that may be, certain events have occurred which have left their traces—prophecies have been uttered which we know to have been fulfilled. How can you explain this, my dear doctor, that a blow given by a spectre shall leave a black mark or bruise on the body of the living being who is the recipient, or how do you explain that events may be pourtrayed in a dream ten, twenty, or even thirty years before that event has taken place. How can that which has no existence inflict an injury? or how foretell things to come?"

"Ah," said the doctor, "you are speaking of the King of Sweden's dream?"

"No—I am speaking of what I have seen myself at Saint Denis, in 1794, at the period of the profanation of the cemeteries."

"Let us hear it," said M. Ledru.

In 1793 I was made director of the museum of French monuments, and in that capacity I was present at the exhumation of the dead in the Abbey of Saint Denis, a name which the enlightened patriots of the day had changed into that of Franciade. Though forty years have elapsed since that day, I can well remember an event which signalised that profanation of all that was sacred.

The intense hatred which had sprung up against royalty in the person of Louis XVI., and which his blood shed on the scaffold on the 21st of January failed to appease, had passed from the king to his family: they wished to pursue monarchy to its very source—having killed the living monarch, they wished to glut their vengeance on the dead—they resolved to scatter to the winds the ashes of sixty kings. Something, too, of curiosity to see the vast treasures said to have been buried in the tombs of the kings, was perhaps mixed with their wish to uproot the vestiges of monarchy. But whatever the motive, the populace flowed like a torrent on to the sepulcre of Saint Denis; and, from the 6th to the 8th of August, they had destroyed fifty-one tombs,—the historical monuments of twelve centuries were annihilated in two days. Then the government of the day resolved to introduce some sort of regularity in this spoliation; they resolved to desecrate the tombs on their own account—as the executors of that monarchy which they had struck to the earth.

Poor fools! they could not understand that, however the efforts of man may sometimes affect the future, he is powerless as to the past.

They had dug in the cemetery an immense pit,—a sort of monster paupers' grave. Into this pit, covered with a layer of quicklime, were thrown the bones of those who had made France the first among nations—from the time of Dagobert to the 15th Louis. In this manner not only was satisfaction afforded to the populace, but, above all, a great source of rejoicing

was given to the furious legislators, the needy advocates, and the snarling, yelping, envious scribblers,—all revolutionary birds of prey, whose eyes were wounded with any show of splendour, decency, or respect—just as those of their brother birds of night are wounded with the broad bright sunshine of heaven; to destroy is the greatest happiness of those who have not the ability to organize or construct.

I was nominated inspector of the exhumations. As the situation would afford me the opportunity of saving many a precious relic from the hands of these Vandals, I accepted it.

On Sunday, the 12th October, we began by opening the vaults of the Bourbons, in the subterranean chapel; and the first operation was to open the coffin of Henry, who, at the age of 57, died by the hands of an assassin, on the 14th of May, 1610. By the bye, I may here mention that the statue erected to his memory on the Pont Neuf, the masterwork of John of Bologne and his students, had been melted down to make two-sous pieces. The body of Henry IV. was in an excellent state of preservation; his features, known as well from the souvenirs of a nation's love, as from the pencil of Rubens, were perfectly recognisable. When the populace saw him taken from his tomb, and beheld him in his shroud, it was only an instinctive respect for the place which prevented them from shouting the once popular cry "Vive Henri IV." I was delighted with these marks of respect, and in order to give full scope to it and their desire to view the remains, I placed the body upright against one of the columns. He was dressed, as while living, in a pourpoint of black velvet, from which the ruff and white lace sleeves had broken away, silk stockings covered his legs and black velvet shoes his feet. His long flowing grey hair formed as it were a halo round the venerated features: and a long silky white beard fell down on his chest.

A procession was organised, similar to that usual at the shrine of a saint; women came and touched the hem of his mantle; others kissed his hands, whilst others made their infants kneel on the ground with themselves, murmuring in a low voice: 'Ah! if he had been living, poor people would not be so unhappy as they are." They might with equal truth have added: 'Nor so ferocious,' for from the bloodthirstiness of the people arose their misery. However, the processions continued for the next two days, namely the Sunday and Monday. On the last-named day the exhumations were renewed. The first body which was brought to the glare of day, after that of Henry IV., was that of his son, Louis XIII. It was in a tolerable state of preservation, and though his features were considerably effaced by decay, his moustache in itself sufficed for recognition. Next came forth the body of Louis XIV., remarkable from those peculiar characteristics of feature which have made his visage the type of the Bourbon family: his body was black as ink. Following him came the corpses of Marie de Medicis, second wife of Henry IV.; of Anne of Austria, wife of Louis XIII.; of Marie Theresa, infanta of Spain, and wife of Louis XIV.; and

of the Grand Dauphin—the whole of these corpses were in a state of putrefaction—that of the Dauphin was a semi-liquid mass.

On Tuesday, the 15th October, the desecration continued: the corpse of Henry IV. was still upright, supported by a column—an impassible participator, as it were, in the vast sacrilege which was being perpetrated on the remains of his descendants.

On Wednesday, the 16th, at the moment when the Queen Marie Antoinette was being beheaded at the Place de la Revolution;—about one o'clock—they had taken from the vault of the Bourbons the coffin of Louis XV.; on opening the coffin, the body seemed, wrapped as it was in bandages and cerecloth, well preserved: but on detaching these, there was visible only the most hideous phase of putrefaction—the horrid effluvium which escaped from it obliged every one to fly the spot: and they were obliged to fire many pounds of gunpowder in order to purify the air. The remains of the heroes of the Parc-au-Cerfs, of the lover of Madame de Chateauroux, of Madame de Pompadour, of Madame du Barry, were all thrown pell-mell into the common grave,—on a bed of quick lime, and covered by a layer of the same, now reposed the remains of those who in their lives were without shame.

I had stopped to arrange the fires and to superintend the laying on of the lime, when on a sudden I heard a tremendous noise in the church. I ran quickly there, and the first thing I saw was a working man at high words with his companions, whilst a crowd of females were pointing at him with their fingers or menacing

The Vision in the Tomb of St. Denis.

him with clenched hands and threatening language.

The miserable wretch had left the horrible occupation in which he had been engaged to witness a spectacle more horrible still—the execution of Marie Antoinette; then, intoxicated by the bloodthirsty cries around him, and in the utterance of which he had joined, infuriated by the sight of the blood he had seen shed on the scaffold, he had hastened back to St. Denis. Rushing to the spot where the remains of Henry IV. rested against the pillar, surrounded by the inquisitive crowd, he addressed the corpse thus :—

"What right hast thou to stand here, when they are cutting off royal heads in the Place de la Revolution ?"

Uttering these words, he caught hold of the dead man's beard with one hand, whilst with the other he struck the corpse a heavy blow on the cheek; it fell to the earth, on which it rattled like a sack of dried bones.

A cry of execration arose on all sides. To any other king the populace perhaps might not have resented such an outrage, but to Henry IV., the people's king, it was considered as an insult to the majesty of the people. Thus the sacrilegious labourer, at the period when I entered the church, ran very great risk of his life. He caught sight of me as I entered, and instantly put himself under my protection. But though I accorded this much, I had no wish to lessen the sense of infamy which the atrocity so well deserved.

"My boys," said I to the labourers, "let this miserable being alone: God will not fail to visit his crime with merited punishment."

So saying, I took the hair from the wretched being's hands which he had torn from the head of the dead king, and replaced it in the coffin. I ordered the fellow out of the edifice, at the same time giving him to understand that he would no longer be employed there. He went forth, followed by the execrations and threats of the people.

Fearing some new outrage against the inanimate corpse, I had it removed to the common grave : in which it was deposited with as much respect as could be shewn.

Evening set in; the workmen had retired, and the sexton alone remained. He was an old, but a brave man, whom I had placed in his office in order to guard against any attempt at new mutilations—or rather sacrilegious robbery : and he accordingly watched from seven at night till seven in the morning, passing the time by patrolling the chapel or sitting by a fire lit at the base of one or other of the pillars.

Everything in this magnificent church bore the emblems of death and destruction. The open vaults, the stones from the top of which were reared against the massive pillars—the fragments of carved work and statuary which strewed the pavement;—the empty coffins, which had given up dead whom the survivors had fondly dreamt would never have been disturbed but by the last trumpet—all these objects excited in the educated mind profound meditation; whilst it struck horror to the feeble and illiterate. But the old church keeper had no thought for the sublime or terrific—he saw in those traces of desecrated humanity nothing but the material debris of broken-up vaults and smashed coffins. It was whilst listening in this unpoetical mood to the slow dull monotonous tolling of the midnight hour from the bell tower of the church, that he heard cries of distress issuing from the cemetery on the outside of the church; he listened—they were renewed—and were plainly heard to be cries for help—followed by those of doleful lamentation. Arming himself with a pick-axe, the old man opened the door leading to the grave yard; here he discovered that the cries proceeded from the grave of the kings: somewhat alarmed, if not frightened, the old man stepped back, shut the door, and ran by the front door to my lodging, which was immediately opposite the church.

I at first refused to pay any attention to the old man's tale; but on listening attentively, after opening my window, I fancied that I did, indeed, hear more than the sound of the wind—in fact, the cries of some one in distress. I therefore arose, and followed him to the cemetery. As we neared the large grave, the cries became feeble—and seemed as if about to cease altogether. Lighting the torches which we brought with us, I directed the man to throw its glare down on the mass of grisly skeletons and putrid corses which were in the pit. He obeyed, and, on looking closely, we caught sight of a man struggling amid the fearful mass: I called out, in a loud voice, "Who are you—and why are you down there?"

"Alas! I am the poor, miserable labourer who struck Henry IV.," was the reply in a weak voice.

"But how came you here?" inquired I.

"Take me out of this, M. Lenoir, for God's sake! and I will tell you all."

Once assured it was a living being who had uttered the cries, the old man knew no fear; and, hastily procuring a ladder which had been laid down amid the rank herbage of the graveyard, he placed it on the bottom of the pit, and descended; here it was discovered that the unfortunate wretch had an arm and a leg broken, so we were obliged to procure a rope, and hoist him up by main strength. No sooner did he reach the top than he fainted. We took him into the church, laid him on straw, near a fire, whilst I despatched the old man for a surgeon, who soon arrived — indeed, the operation of setting the bones was begun before the unfortunate had recovered from his insensibility. The surgeon, having dressed the broken limbs, left; and soon after I dismissed the guardian for the remainder of the night, consequently I was left alone in the church with the wounded man. In fact, I had a great curiosity to know how it was that the man had been thus placed, and how he had met his serious injuries. I, therefore, sat me down on a stone, close to the wounded man; the light from the fire threw its fitful flashes ever and anon on the pain-drawn countenance of the sufferer, and lighting up the immediately surrounding space by gleams which only served to make the darkness of the distant portion of the edifice appear more profound; thus sitting, as I said, I questioned the sufferer, and the following was the substance of his replies:

He stated that, having money in his pocket, and being in no risk of immediate want, dismissal from his employment had troubled him but little : and he had gone from the church to a wine-shop. He had just broached his first bottle, when the landlord accosted him:

"Have you nearly finished your drink?"

"Why?" asked the labourer.

"Because I hear that you are the man who struck the corpse of Henry IV."

"Well—I did so," said the labourer, insolently. "What then?"

"What then!—I have no wish to furnish drink to such a villain as thou art: it would bring a curse on my house."

"Your house is every man's house: and, whilst I pay for what I drink, I am at home."

"But you shall not pay at all," said the innkeeper.

"And why not?"

"Because I will not take your money. So, my fine fellow, as you don't pay, you are not in your own house—but in mine; and as I don't like your company, I shall show you the way to the door."

"Yes—if you are able."

"If I am not, I will call others to assist me."

"Call away—I should like to see them."

The innkeeper did call: and three stout-limbed stablemen came: the labourer, seeing the odds were against him—much as he wished for a quarrel, thought it best to take a summary leave. After straying about the town, at the dinner hour he repaired to a low eating-house, frequented by men of his own grade. Here he had no sooner commenced his repast than he was again recognised; and one of the company, stepping up to the proprietor, informed him it was the universal determination of him and his companions, never to again come into his house if that man was allowed to eat his dinner there.

"Why—what has he done?" said the shop-keeper.

"That's the fellow who knocked down the corpse of Henry IV."

"Out of this!" said the enraged housekeeper, striding up to the poor devil, "I wish what thou hast eaten may poison thee."

If there was small chance of resisting three men, there was still less of resisting twenty. So, rising from his seat, and venting loud and deep imprecations on everybody and everything, he again took to the streets: where he roamed, cursing and blaspheming, until night, when, hungry, thirsty, weary, and furious, he took his way to his lodgings. On knocking at the door, the lodging-house keeper looked from an upper window, and asked who was there?"

The labourer gave his name.

"Ah!" said the housekeeper, "You are the fellow who struck Henry IV. Wait a bit."

"What the devil am I to wait for?" growled the vagabond. Scarce had he uttered the words when a somewhat clumsily packed-up parcel nearly knocked him into the road.

"There—now you have everything belonging to you that was in my house. Now go and lodge where you can. I have no fancy to bring the roof of my house on my head."

A stone through the window, narrowly escaping the speaker's head, was the response of the enraged labourer. This was followed, on the part of the lodging-house keeper, by loud calls for the lodgers to rise and assist; on which, the disowned of all men took his departure from the house with his usual quota of hard words; and, finding the door of a shed open about a hundred yards distant, he lay down on some straw, and was soon asleep. He supposed it must have been near midnight when it appeared to him that some one touched him on the shoulder. He awoke, and saw a female in white, who beckoned him to follow her. Believing her to be some one of those unfortunates who have a bed for any poor vagabond who has the means to pay, and, having money with him, and at the same time preferring taking his rest in a bed rather than on the rough couch of straw, he arose from his lair and followed the woman, who walked for some moments along the high street, and then dived down a narrow lane,—still making signs for the labourer to follow. As the direction she took led to the quarter where the dwellings of those abandoned to vice abounded, he felt no repugnance in following her steps, until he found himself in the fields. Accounting for this by supposing that the woman dwelt in some isolated cottage, he still followed—until, passing through a breach in a ruined wall, he found himself in the graveyard of the Abbey of St. Denis,—the windows of which were lighted up from within as if for some grand spectacle or service. Turning

to seek an explanation from the female, he found she had disappeared. He turned to retrace his steps, but in the breach of the wall through which he had entered, stood, in a menacing attitude, the spectre of Henry IV. He started back, and the spectre advanced—face to face they stood—step by step the spectre pursued—step by step the labourer retreated. All at once the ground slipped away from under his feet, and he fell headlong into the immense grave of the kings. Here, it appeared to him as if were assembled the whole of the royalty of France—the predecessors and descendants of the outraged monarch—some lifted on high their sceptres—others held aloft the mace of justice—and all cried aloud for vengeance on the wretch who had committed the double crime of sacrilege and disloyalty. Then, as if with one fell crash, the sceptres and maces were hurled on his frame—and fell like burning flames on his limbs—he found his arm and leg broken—and it was then that the fearful cry of agony which burst from him had aroused the watchman. This was the purport of his story. I did all I could to reassure the unhappy wretch; but his mind was past all comprehension but upon one subject, and he died in a few hours, crying for pardon for his crime.

"You will excuse me," said the doctor, "but really I cannot see the connection between the story you have just recited, and the premises with which you prefaced it. The accident which happened to this unfortunate labourer was purely the natural result of a mind exasperated, tortured, combined with the harassing bodily discomforts of hunger, thirst, and weariness. Influenced by these, his mind had wandered—he had passed into a state of somnambulism, and had unconsciously traced his steps to the abbey graveyard—he had there fallen into the pit, and, in his fall, broken his limbs. All this I can understand: but I can see no prediction realised —not a shadow of it."

"Wait for the sequel, doctor," said the chevalier, "you shall have a prediction which was verified to the letter—and which is, as I maintain, mysterious.

It was about the 20th January, 1794, after the demolition of the tomb of Francis I., that they opened the vault of the Comtesse of Flanders, wife of Philip the Tall; and these two were the last of the royal vaults which remained for spoliation—every tomb had been broken open; every grave had been emptied—every bone consigned to the common charnel-house. For the last time, the old watchman guarded the church—alas! there was now little but the bare walls to guard: he had, therefore, obtained permission to sleep, if he chose, and he lost no time in profiting by this consent. Towards midnight he was awakened from his sleep by the deep diapason of the vast organ, and the chanting of monks. He awoke, rubbed his eyes to discover if he was awake, and turning his head towards the choir from whence the tones proceeded, he was astonished at the gorgeous spectacle which there met his gaze. There were the seats of the choir filled by the monks of the Abbey of St. Denis, in all the plenitude of their saintly garb; the archbishop in his robes was

L'Artifia l'e.

officiating at the high altar; the chapel royal was lit up as on state occasions in the palmy days of monarchy; and hung with the cloth of black velvet and gold, which was only used on the occasion of deaths in the royal family of France. Grand mass had apparently just been finished as he awoke, and the ceremony usual at royal funerals had just commenced.

The sceptre, the crown, and the mace of justice, laid on a cushion of crimson velvet, were taken from the heralds, and put into the hands of three princes of the blood royal. Immediately gliding, as it were, rather than walking, for no sound of footstep echoed along the vaulted aisles, the gentlemen of the presence chamber took the coffin and deposited it in the vault of the Bourbon family. Then the king-at-arms descended into the vault; and cried to the heralds to come forward and do their offices.—The first herald descended into the vault and deposited on the coffin the royal spurs; the second deposited the gauntlets; the third, the sword: the fourth, the royal crest; and the fifth and last, the coat of arms. In turn the herald proceeded to call the first valet of the king, who carried the royal banner, the captain of the Swiss Guard, the archer of the Royal Guard, and the two hundred gentlemen of the royal household; the first chamberlain, carrying the banner of France; the grand master of the

The Abbé and the Burglar.

household, before whom all the deputy masters filed, throwing their broken wands of office into the royal vault, saluting the three princes of the blood who bore the royal insignia,—and, finally, the three princes themselves. Then the king-at-arms cried twice in a loud voice,—

"The king is dead! Long live the king."

A herald in the choir repeated the cry. Then the grand master of the household, breaking his wand across his knee, threw the pieces into the royal vault: Immediately the trumpets sounded ; the organ was again pealing forth its deep music through the gothic aisles— and whilst the trumpets seemed to sound fainter, and the sonorous strains of the organ seemed to subside into the low wail of departed souls,

the lights gradually faded, the forms and features of the attendants melted into their shadows, and as the last faint whisper of the music died on the ear, the whole vision disappeared from the eye, leaving nought but the moonbeam throwing its pale rays uninterrupted but by the vast pillars and arching roof.

Such was the tale related to me by the old watchman—who was moved to tears whilst describing it—of the royal interment which he had, he said, seen with his own waking eyes ; and which he believed an infallible revelation to him that the desecrated tombs and royal relics should be replaced and restored to their pristine honours—and, in spite of all the decrees of the Convention, or the massacres by the guillotine, France should have a new monarchy and St. Denis fresh occupants of its royal vaults. This revelation, however, being bruited about, had very nearly brought the prophet's head to the scaffold. Thirty years afterwards, on the 21st of September, 1824, I was leaning against the very column of the abbey against which the old man had been reclining when he saw this strange vision—when a very old man pulled me by the sleeve of my coat—

"Well," said the man to me. "When I told you that our poor kings should one day come back to Saint Denis, was I not right?"

In fact, he was: for on that day was interred in the royal vault the remains of Louis XVIII., and with the same ceremony and pomp which had so struck the old watchman in his vision thirty years before, in the bloodiest days of the Revolution.

Explain that, doctor.

CHAPTER X.

MYSTERY VI.—L'ARTIFIAILLE.

WHETHER it was because he was convinced, or whether—by far the most probable idea—he thought it rather a difficult matter to give a negative to the opinions of a man like the chevalier, the doctor was silent. This silence of course left the field of discussion open to others; and the Abbé Moulle rushed into the arena.

"All this only confirms me in my own system," said he.

"And what may be your system?" said the doctor, delighted at the chance of having a tilt with gentler jousters than M. Ledru or the chevalier.

"That we live under the influence of two invisible worlds—peopled, the one with infernal spirits, the other with celestial; that from the hour of our birth a good and bad genius is ever attendant on us—accompanies us through life, even to the gates of eternity: ever the one is whispering the counsels of goodness, benevolence, and all which tends to make man the reflection of the godhead from whom his spirit emanates; incessantly is our evil genius pouring into our mind's ear the suggestions of vice, and placing before our eyes its allurements and seductions; and, finally, the victory is achieved either by the one or the other—either our soul becomes the prey of a demon or the habitation of an angel. So, in the case of the poor Solange, it was her good genius which, by the lips of the young martyr, muttered her everlasting adieus to M. Ledru; while, in the case of the burglar sentenced by the Scottish judge, the demon remained master: and it was this evil spirit which came successively as a cat, an usher, and a skeleton. In the last case, it was the good genius of the monarchy which revenged on the brutal labourer the indignity committed on its representative, and finally revealed to the humble night-watch the restoration of the fallen monarchy, and its resuscitation with all the

pomp and circumstance which could have emblazoned the ceremonies of the court of Louis XIII."

"But you will agree that everything must be founded upon conviction?" said the doctor.

"Doubtless."

"But this conviction, in order to be real, must be founded on a fact."

"It is upon a fact that my conviction is based."

"On a fact which has been related to you by a person of unimpeachable veracity?"

"I allude to a fact which happened to myself—which is of my own knowledge."

"Give us your facts, then?" said the doctor.

"With pleasure," replied the abbé, and proceeded as follows:

I was born on that part of the territory of ancient France which used to be called the Department de l'Aisne, and sometimes styled the Isle of France; my parents dwelt in a little village, situate in the centre of the forest of Villars-Cotterets, and which is called Fleury. I was the last of five children, all of whom, myself excepted, had died in their infancy. From this circumstance, my mother, previously to my birth, had dedicated me to the Virgin Mary, and my father had vowed to take, on my birth, a pilgrimage to Our Lady of Liesse—a religious custom procedure which was, in similar cases, not unfrequent in the old-fashioned provinces of France. Unfortunately, my father died suddenly during my mother's pregnancy, but this did not deter my mother from the performance of the engagement she had entered into; at my birth I was habited in white from head to foot, and, as soon as I could walk, my mother, not content with her own part of the vows made on my behalf, undertook the pilgrimage vowed by my deceased father; this, by the way, was not such an affair as a pilgrimage to Rome or Loretto, as Our Lady of Liesse was but sixty or seventy miles from our village. Thanks to this double guarantee, I passed safely through the years of childhood and adolescence—and, whether it was the effect of the religious education I had received, or that of the medal which my mother had received as a token of the accomplishment of my father's vows, and which I had invariably worn around my neck, I certainly felt an ardent attachment to the priesthood. Having finished my studies at Soissons, I was ordained priest in 1780, and was sent as a vicar to Etampes, and it so happened that the church to which I was nominated was one of the four in Etampes which was dedicated to Our Lady. It was one of those remarkable monuments bequeathed by the first centuries of Christianity to the middle ages. Founded by Robert the Strong, it was not finished until the second century, and to this day the rare and valuable stained glass windows of its pristine period remain, and, since the re-construction of the sacred edifice, harmonize well with its paintings and the ornamental carvings which cover its columns from base to the capital. Even whilst a child I was greatly in love with those marvellous granite structures with which the piety of the tenth and the following centuries had covered our fair land of France—Rome's eldest son—and which was only checked when the true faith died away from the hearts of the people, killed by the poisonous tenets of Luther and Calvin. I had played, whilst a child, in the ruins of Saint John of Soissons; I had feasted my eyes on its richly carved efflorescence,—its quaint corbels, and the lofty spring of its arched roof;—and it was no small happiness to me, with those feelings engrafted on my heart, to find myself like a swallow, in such a nest; or, halcyon like, to brood in pensive meditation in its calm and placid aisles. Indeed, the happiest moments of my life were spent in this church. I will not assert that the sentiment with which I was thus imbued was one purely religious: my sensations might perhaps be compared to those of a bird whom some experimental philosopher has taken from the exhausted receiver of an air-pump, and restored to the world and liberty.—My world was circumscribed by the walls of the church: my liberty was to kneel at some tomb, or lean, wrapt in sweet meditation, against one of the pillars. And on what subject were my reveries? Certainly they did not relate to theological dogmas, synodical subtleties, or the decretals of general councils; no,—my thoughts were invariably plunged into speculations regarding the eternal struggle between the powers of good and evil; now indulging in phantastical imaginings of white-robed angel visitants,—now gloomily conning over the vague horrors—physical and spiritual—which are attributed to the doomed spirits; and these thoughts were not a little heightened by constant gazing at the many-tinted scenes depicted in the stained-glass window, and the quaint and fantastic demonology with which the architect had decorated the corbels. In this church I dwelt—I thought —I prayed; and the midnight hour had often broken on the still night and vibrated through the moon lit aisles and lofty arches of the edifice ere I had quitted it for my couch.

Enclosed as I was in an atmosphere of my own, shut out from the world, and living almost as if having no interest beyond the narrow bounds of my sacred study, very few events of the outer world reached my ear, or attracted my attention. Still there was one event which penetrated even my hermitage—it had long been known to clergy and laity. The vicinity of Etampes had long suffered from the depredations of a burglar—a successor if not a rival to Cartouche or De Poullailler; indeed his success and audacity seemed to surpass even those of his famed predecessors.

But perhaps there was one circumstance which tended more to attract my attention towards this criminal than even the fact of his having been the perpetrator of several sacrileges in the churches around: and this was the fact that the criminal's wife was one of my most devout penitents. A most worthy and pious woman, allied to the most hardened and irreclaimable criminals, she strove, as it were, by her good works, to extenuate the offences of her husband,—who, steeped in crime to his very hair—neither fearing God nor devil, was of opinion that society was badly organised—that he was sent on purpose to correct its evils, and restore the balance to equality and community— in fact, he might have been said to have been the precursor of certain political fanatics whom we have seen spring up in our own time under the name of Socialist. Five several times had this criminal been shut up within the walls of a prison; and as many times had he contrived to elude the vigilance of his keepers, and regain his liberty: indeed the peasantry had a silly belief that he had become the owner of a wonderful secret—that of a herb powerful enough to sever iron bolts and bars: consequently, there was an air of the marvellous which attached to his exploits. I had, as I have hinted before, become aware of the culprit's delinquencies through the agony of his poor wife while at confession: I gave her the best advice I could, but all her endeavours to reclaim him were of no avail.

Easter, 1783, was at hand. On the day before the Good Friday preceding that festival, I had been more than ordinarily fatigued with the labour of the confessional: so much so, that at 8 o'clock I fell asleep there. The sacristan had observed me, but knowing my habits, and that I had a key which could at any time open the church door, he took no notice. I slept on till near midnight: when I awoke I heard the clock striking the hour—I fancied also I heard footsteps on the pavement. I was about to leave the confessional, when by a bright gleam of moonlight streaming through the stained windows I saw a man cross the chapel; and I inferred from the precautions he took in passing the various objects and his looking around him ever and anon, that he was not one of those whose duties were connected with the services of the church, but some one to whom the place was unfamiliar, and of whose intentions in entering the church at midnight I augured ill. My nocturnal visitor proceeded to the choir, where, having struck a light, he lit a wax taper from the altar. By this light I saw a man of middle height, armed with pistols and a poignard; his features had much more of a scoffing, sneering expression, than of the terrible: he looked anxiously around as soon as he had achieved his light, and the examination seemed satisfactory, for a grim smile passed over his coarse features. Losing no time in deliberation, he immediately drew from his pocket a bundle of picklocks, and by the aid of one of these instruments soon succeeded in opening the tabernacle, taking from it the pix, a magnificent silver cup of the time of the second Henry, a silver oil-cruet, and two plated flagons—in fact, all that the tabernacle contained. The shrine below the altar was next opened and its contents taken out; here was a representation of the Virgin, in wax, the head surmounted by a crown of gold, and the vestments embroidered with diamonds and precious stones: and the thief was making up the different articles into one parcel, when I, fully satisfied as to his intentions, came forth from the confessional, and made my way towards the altar. The noise of my footsteps disturbed the robber in his employment: and I could see him eagerly and anxiously peering into the darkness in order to discover who it was that was in the church. As soon as he perceived me, he rose, took a pistol from his belt, and presented it at my head. A second glance convinced

The Abbé absolving the Burglar's Wife.

him that I was but a helpless inoffensive priest,—with no defence save that of my faith, no weapon save that of the word of God. Notwithstanding the menacing attitude of the robber, I advanced calmly towards him: I felt no fear—and, therefore, betrayed no symptoms of perturbation. My tranquillity appeared to have some effect on the burglar: for his voice betrayed emotion as he called out:—

"What do you want?"

"You are L'Artifiaille," said I to him.

"Parbleu; who else would dare to break into a church alone and unassisted?"

"Poor hardened sinner, that pride yourself on crime, know you not that you are playing a game by which you will not only lose your life, but your precious soul?"

"Bah!" said he, "I have saved my carcase many times, and hope to do so again; as for my soul—why just look at my wife: she has piety enough for both of us, and she can save my soul at the same time she is saving her own."

"You say truly," I said, "that your wife is a pious woman; and she will certainly die with grief if she should discover that you had committed the crime you are now perpetrating."

"Ah—ah! you really believe that my poor wife will die of grief."

"I am certain of it," I replied.

"I shall be a jolly widower then," replied the burglar, laughing loudly, at the same time putting forth his hands to resume his occupation of packing up the spoil.

I made three steps towards the altar, and arrested his arm, saying—

"No! you shall not commit this sacrilege."

Page 60.

"Who will hinder me?" he enquired.

"I will."

"How?"

"Not by force. God has not sent his servant armed with the might of physical force,—which is a thing altogether of the earth—but endowed with the heavenly power of persuasion. My friend, it is not so much on account of the church —which could procure other paraphernalia— that I would hinder you from committing this sin, but it is for your sake that I interfere. My friend, you may not commit this crime."

"Perhaps you fancy it is the first I have committed?"

"No—I know that, unhappily, it is not your first—nor tenth—nor, perhaps, twentieth sacri-lege. But then you were blind to the enormity of your crime,—now your eyes are opened. Have you not heard of Saul, who guarded the clothes of those who stoned the holy St. Stephen? Well, this young man's eyes were blinded, until the scales fell from his eyes—he saw, and this young man was afterwards Saint Paul."

"St. Paul—did they not crucify him?"

"Yes."

"Well, what availed his good sight, if he could not see how to escape his doom?"

"It will serve to convince you, my friend, that salvation sometimes comes from suffering and death. To this day, the name of St. Paul is venerated on earth, and his soul is revelling in beatitude."

"How old was St. Paul."

"About thirty."

"Ah! I'm forty—I am too old to change."

"It is never too late for repentance," said I, and I instanced the thief on the cross.

"There—that's all very well, I dare say. But," said the burglar, looking at me hardly, "do you mean to hold on to the silver?"

"No—I would hold on to your crime-steeped soul, for I wish earnestly to save it from perdition."

"Oh! you only care for my soul—you don't gammon badly."

"Shall I prove the truth of my assertion?" said I.

"Rather a hard matter," he replied, with a sneer.

"At what sum do you estimate the profits of the crime you intended to commit to-night?"

"Well," replied the thief, looking around and scanning with a practised eye the articles of value that he had collected and made ready for removal, "I should say it would bring me in about a thousand crowns."

"A thousand crowns?"

"Oh, I know very well the things are worth double that sum, but those devils of jews are such thieves I shall lose two-thirds of their value."

"Come to my house?"

"To your house!"

"Yes, come home with me to the vicarage, I have there a thousand francs, which I will give you on account."

"And how about the other two thousand?"

"Well, I promise you, on the faith of a priest, that I will pay you all. I will go home to my place of birth: my mother has some property there, and I will sell three or four acres of land to procure the remainder of the thousand crowns—these I will give you."

"Exactly; you will be kind enough to give me a rendezvous, so that I may nicely put my head into a noose."

"You are saying that which you do not really believe," said I looking him sternly in the face.

"Well—well—perhaps you are right," he replied, sullenly. "Is your mother very rich?"

"On the contrary, she is poor."

"She would be ruined, then?"

"When I tell her that the price of that ruin may be the gain of an immortal soul, she will bless me for it. Besides, when she has lost all, she can live with me at the vicarage; I shall have enough for us both."

"Agreed," said he, "I will go with you."

"Very well—but stay—one thing remains for you to do."

"What is that?"

"Replace the sacred things you have taken—shut and lock them up in their proper receptacles."

"The frown on the brow of the burglar, whilst complying with my request, showed the internal struggle which it cost him to give up his spoil.

"Come on," said he.

"In the next place, you must make the sign of the cross," I said.

He tried to laugh, but the smile died away, and, after a moment's hesitation, he obeyed.

"Now, follow me."

We left the church, and repaired to my house, the burglar looking around in an uneasy anxious manner, from time to time, as if fearing some ambuscade. On reaching the door, he exclaimed:

"Now let me have the thousand francs?"

"Wait a moment," I replied. I went to my room, and returned to him with a bag containing the amount.

"There it is," said I to him, as I gave him the money.

"But when shall I have the remainder?" asked the thief.

"You must wait six weeks."

"Very well; I'll give you six weeks."

"To whom am I to give this money?" asked I.

After a moment's reflection, he answered me: "Send it to my wife; but, understand this, she must not know who sends it, or the manner in which it was got."

"I promise that; but, on my side, I must insist that you promise never to attempt a sacrilege again in the church of our Lady of Etampes, or in any other church dedicated to the Virgin."

"I promise you I will not attempt it."

"On your word?"

"On the faith of L'Artifaille."

"Go, my friend, and sin no more," said I—making him a sign to retire. He hesitated a moment, then, opening the door quietly, he went out. Left to myself, I fell on my knees, and breathed a prayer for the unhappy criminal. I had scarce finished and risen from my orisons, when I was startled by a knock at the door. I opened the door, and immediately perceived the burglar standing before me.

"Here," said he, at the same time holding out the money in his hand, "I have brought back your thousand francs, and I shall hold you quits as to the remainder."

"And what as to the promise you have made me?"

"I hold to that."

"You repent, then, of your crime?"

"I know not whether I do or do not repent: all I know is, that I will not have a farthing of your money," and, so saying, he placed the money-bag on the sideboard.

Seeing that he remained silent, but seemed desirous of communicating something which he had not resolution enough to utter, I asked him what he wished me to do. "Say on, my friend," said I, "do not be ashamed of doing well."

"You have a profound veneration for our Lady?" he asked, in a low tone of voice.

"Very great, indeed," I replied.

"And you believe that, by her intercession, a being so heinously guilty as I am might be pardoned at the last hour. Well, in exchange for the three thousand francs, which I give back to you, give me some relique, some rosary, or chaplet—anything sacred, in short, which I may press to my lips in my last hour?"

Detaching the medal which I had worn round my neck from the day of my birth, and which, up to that moment, had never quitted its resting place, I gave it to the burglar, who pressed it to his lips, and fled from the house.

A twelvemonth passed away, and I heard nothing respecting L'Artifaille, and I had no doubt that he had quitted Etampes to exercise his predatory habits elsewhere. Meanwhile, I received a letter from my *confrère*, the vicar of Fleury, informing me of the illness of my mother. I obtained leave of absence, and remained there for five or six weeks, until the happy restoration of my mother to health enabled me to return to my duties.

I arrived at Etampes on a Friday afternoon; I found the village in a commotion. The famous L'Artifaille had been retaken near Orleans, had been tried, condemned, and sent back to Etampes to be hung in pursuance of his sentence; this was done, the execution having taken place on the morning of my arrival. All this I heard before I entered my house; on reaching the vicarage, I was informed that a female of the lower town had been at the vicarage every morning and every evening since the arrival of L'Artifaille, anxiously asking if I was at home, and when I should return. I knew of no woman of the lower town save one—the newly made widow of the condemned and executed criminal. I resolved to go to her immediately, even before resting from the fatigue of my journey home. I therefore, went into the faubourg, and the house being indicated to me, I found the outer door open, and walked in. Through the small window of the inner door I saw a woman kneeling at the foot of a bed, and, by the violent agitation of her shoulders, I saw that she was sobbing hysterically. On my knocking at the door, she arose and opened it.

"Oh, Monsieur l'Abbé," she exclaimed, "my heart told me it was you. Alas! alas! you have come too late—too late! my husband is dead, and died without having confessed."

"Did he die, then, in hardness of heart?"

"No, no; on the contrary, thanks to the Blessed Virgin, I am sure he died a Christian in his heart: but he declared solemnly he would confess to no priest but yourself—and, that if he did not confess to you, he would only confess to the Holy Virgin. And whilst saying this, he repeatedly took from his breast a little medal, which he kissed, and begged me to take care that the medal should not be taken from him, adding that if the medal was buried with him, the Evil One would have no power over him."

"Is that all he said?"

"No: on the way to the scaffold, he told me you would be home to-night, that I was to see you immediately on your arrival—this is why I have been at your house so many times to-day. Yes: and he charged me to make to you one last request. He charged me, that immediately I saw you I was to ask you to—ah! my God—I dare not ask such a thing for him—"

"Say on, my good woman—say on."

"That I should beg of you to go to the place of execution, and there, under his body, to repeat, for the good of his soul, five *paters* and five *aves*."

"I will go there to-night."

"Oh—you are a good man!" said the poor woman, kissing my hands.

Disengaging my hands, I said to her, "Be of good courage, my good woman, and if what my poor efforts can do will bring repose to his soul, it shall be gladly accorded. So saying, I left the house.

It was now half-past ten at night, and the north-east wind blew piercingly, for it was the month of April. The moon, shining fitfully at intervals, betwixt masses of dark, heavy, threatening clouds, which scudded at a swift pace through the air, gave a dismal though picturesque horizon. I walked as quickly as I could through the town, passing out by the gate on the road to Paris. The place of execution was a sort of esplanade—anciently a fortified place which commanded the town, but nought now remained of its defences, save two or three fragments of masonry, which served as supports to the uprights of the grim and ghastly gallows, which loomed dimly through the murky air. In order to reach this place, I had to pass under the frowning tower of Guinnette—a fortification which served as an advanced work to the esplanade, and which Louis XI. had in vain attempted to blow into the air: at this moment it is the habitation of the raven by day, and the palace of the owl by night: from this place I proceeded by a narrow and rugged path, cut out of the rock, and lined on each side with brambles. Not a sound was to be heard around save the monotonous click-clack of the old mill in the village below,—the hootings of the owl, and the rustling of the wind among the bushes. I had no fear, but I had that undefinable anxious sensation which sometimes invades our minds prior to an extraordinary event: and it was with a shudder that I first caught sight of the condemned man, swinging in the night wind, the moon ever and anon throwing its calm and silvery light on the ghastly lineaments. Whilst my eyes were rivetted for a moment on the horrid spectacle, I perceived something moving at the foot of the gallows, which at the distance I was seemed to be some four-footed animal: it appeared larger than a wolf and higher than a dog. Whilst I was gazing in mute terror, on a sudden the supposed quadruped assumed a posture which immediately convinced me that the animal was of the genius *homo*,—or, as Plato would have described it, a two-legged unfeathered animal, alias man.

What could bring a man, at that time of night, to the foot of a gibbet? I could only divine two motives—one was to pray for the unhappy malefactor—the other with some criminal design. In this incertitude, I determined to watch the actions of this midnight visitor: so, placing myself behind a rock which jutted out into the path, I kept my eyes fixed on the base of the gallows. The moon now emerged from behind a dark mass of clouds into the clear open sky—and I could see clearly that the man, having procured a ladder from the vicinage, placed it against the scaffold, and immediately mounted it. An instant after, the living and the dead semed as if in an embrace—so closely were they together. Utterly confounded, I was about to emerge from my hiding-place, when I was horrified at hearing a cry of mortal anguish proceed from the scaffold. I saw two bodies swinging in the air—I heard half-stifled shrieks for help, becoming more and more inarticulate;

PREUHOMME

and, finally, I saw one of the two bodies fall from the beam to the earth, leaving the other suspended in the air in the horrible convulsions of death by strangulation.

Although it was utterly impossible for me to understand the strange proceedings taking place before my eyes, I could not withstand an appeal for succour under such circumstances : and in another moment I had reached the scaffold, mounted the ladder, and with one cut of my knife, severed the cord by which the man was hanging ; he fell heavily to the earth, by the side of the body which had at first dropped from the scaffold. With some trouble I disengaged the knot from the neck of the last suspended—and thus gaining a nearer view of his features—disfigured and horrible as they were from half

strangulation and mortal agony—I recognised in them the hangman. After a few minutes of painful and laboured respiration, he began to breathe more freely ; I placed him in a sitting position against a stone, and soon had the satisfaction of seeing him open his eyes, and stare wildly about him. His astonishment seemed to be quite bewildering when he recognised me.

"Oh !—oh !—M. l'Abbé—is that you ?"

"Yes, it is I."

"What brought—you here ?" he asked.

"I ought to ask that of you."

He seemed to rally his scattered wits. Looking around him a second time, he caught sight of the cold and livid corse at his side.

"Ah !" said he, with a shudder, trying to rise, "let us go, M. l'Abbé—in heaven's name

let us begone from here."

"You can go whenever you please, friend," said I, "but I have a duty to perform."

"Here ?"

I answered affirmatively.

"What have you to do, then ?" enquired the hangman.

"The unhappy man who lies there has exacted a promise that I would repeat certain prayers, at the foot of the scaffold, for the salvation of his soul."

"For the salvation of his soul ! Oh, M. l'Abbé, "you will lose your labour by doing that, for he is the devil himself."

"How ?"

"Not a doubt of it. Did you not see how he served me ? Why he hanged me as neatly as if he had been brought up to the business."

"It appears to me, friend, on the contrary, that it is you have done him that miserable office."

"I' faith, I thought I had done the job completely, but I was deceived. But why the deuce did he not save himself when I was dangling in his place ?"

"Because he was dead," I replied.

"Dead—is he dead ? So much the worse. Let us be off, M. l'Abbé—and save ourselves." So saying, he rose to his feet. But faith, I had better remain where I am, for who knows but what he might get up and run after me. And you, holy man as you are, you will defend me if I stop."

"Friend," said I, looking at him fixedly—"there is something hidden under this mystery. You asked me a little while ago why I came here, I have informed you. I demand to know from you your business at such an hour at this place?"

"Ah! i' faith—I know I must tell you, sooner or later, voluntarily or in confession. Well, I will tell you voluntarily. But stop"—and here he made a retreating movement.

"What is the matter?"

"Did you not fancy he moved?"

"No: you may rest yourself easy on that score. The unfortunate is dead."

"Dead—really dead? No matter. I will tell you why I came here. I will tell you the whole truth—and if I lie I have no doubt he will contradict me. I must tell you that the criminal lying there wished much to confess to you. He would ask, from time to time, if l'Abbé Moulle was come. On being told he was not yet arrived, he would sigh heavily. We brought him a priest, but his only cry was 'L'Abbé Moulle—and no other.' At the foot of the scaffold, he stopped suddenly. 'Is l'Abbé Moulle arrived?' inquired he. 'No,' was the answer. 'Go on,' said he. After the preparations had been all made, he said to me, 'Wait a moment, that I may be certain the abbé is not come.' He gazed anxiously over the vast crowd which was assembled: not seeing you he sighed deeply. Thinking there was nothing more to be done, I was about to push him from the ladder. He saw my intention, and called out 'Wait a moment.' 'What for?' said I. 'I wish to kiss a medal of Our Lady, which I wear round my neck.' 'Very proper,' I replied, 'kiss it by all means;' and I placed the medal against his lips. 'What more do you want?' demanded I. 'I wish this medal to be buried with me!' 'Hem—hem!' I replied; 'it is the custom that all property found on the condemned after execution, is the hangman's perquisite.' 'That doesn't concern me,' said he; 'my medal must be buried with me! I wish—' 'You wish,' said I, losing all patience, and launching him into eternity, 'To the Devil with you and your wishes.'

"But what has all this to do with your coming here at midnight?" I inquired.

"Ah! that's the most difficult part of the affair," said he, hesitatingly.

"Well, I will tell you," said I. "You came here to purloin the dead man's medal."

"True—the Devil tempted me. Well—when night was fairly set in, I started from my house: arrived here, I sought the ladder, which I had hidden close by; to set it against the scaffold and mount it was the work of a moment. I took the body in my arms, and was detaching the chain from its neck, when—

"What?" said I.

"You will scarcely believe what I tell you; but it is true for all that. As soon as I had taken the medal from his neck, the body seized me in its clutches, drew it's head from the noose, and put mine in the place of it: it then pushed me off the ladder, and left me dangling in the air."

"Impossible!" I exclaimed. "You are telling me falsehoods."

"Did you or did you not find me hanging?"

"I did."

"Well—I know well I was not fool enough to hang myself. Now you know all I can tell you of the affair."

I was silent for a moment, and then inquired where the medal was. He informed me that it fell to the earth; for when he felt himself suspended, he let it fall from his hands. After some little search, I discovered it, and immediately put it round the neck of L'Artifaille's corpse. At the moment it touched the breast of the dead man, a trembling seized and ran through all his limbs—and a cry of mingled anguish and despair issued from the corpse. The hangman jumped back in awful terror, trembling like a leaf. I felt no fear, but rather satisfaction and serenity. I called to mind the expulsion of the demons mentioned in Holy Writ, and from my heart I believed this to be a similar case.

"Come here, friend," said I to the terror-stricken wretch near me, "be not afraid."

He complied, hesitatingly. "What is your will?" said he.

"That you immediately put the corpse in its place on the scaffold."

"Never. Do you wish to see me strung up a second time?"

"There is no fear of that: while that medal is on the corpse, you can experience no evil from it."

"Why not?"

"Because that body is under its protection; and the evil spirit by which it was animated and possessed has fled howling from its habitation: it was your dispossessing the body of the medal that enabled the demon to gain occupation. And it is necessary that you should again suspend it, that justice should have its course. Fear nothing, but do your duty."

"Well—but promise me you will not take your eyes from the spot, and that at the least sound you will come to my aid."

"I promise you that."

He approached the corpse: cautiously and tenderly he took the body in his arms, and carried it towards the scaffold, talking to it all the time in a soothing, deprecating style;—

"Don't be afraid, L'Artifaille, they shall not take your medal from you again—You won't let me out of your sight, M. l'Abbé?"

"Make yourself easy. I'll keep my eye on you"

He continued his address to the corpse, in the same bland, conciliatory tone. "We are not going to take the medal—no: it shall be buried with you.—True enough, he does not stir a peg, M. l'Abbé." Then he again resumed his consoling communications to the corpse. "I am going to put you in your own place, you know, at the orders of M. l'Abbé," said he, mounting the ladder

I could scarce refrain from smiling: as the scene had too much of the ludicrous for me, I begged him to be quick.

"It is done," said he: and with one bound he sprang from the ladder to the ground, leaving the corpse swaying in the air.

I fell on my knees, and I was about to commence the prayers I had promised to repeat, when I was interrupted by the hangman, who had fallen on his knees by my side.

"Will M. l'Abbé have the kindness to say

the prayers loud and slow enough for me to hear and repeat them after him?"

"Have you forgotten them?" said I to the wretched man.

"I don't recollect ever learning them," was the reply.

I went through the prayers, which the hangman repeated word for word. Then I said, "L'Arti-faille—I have performed all in my power for your soul's repose: the rest I leave to God."

"Amen," responded my companion.

"Now," said I to the hangman. "We have no more to do here."

"M. L'Abbé," said he, "will you do me a last favour?"

"What is it?"

"Just to escort me to my home; I confess to you that I shall not feel comfortable till I have the door locked between me and that gentleman there."

I consented; and having accompanied him to his home, I reached my own.

When I awoke in the morning, I was informed that the burglar's widow was waiting to speak to me.

I went to her; she appeared with a countenance radiant and joyous.

"M. L'Abbé," said she, "I have come to thank you. My husband appeared to me last night, and said to me, 'To-morrow morning you must go to the Abbé Moulle, and tell him that, thanks to God and to him, I am happy.'"

CHAPTER XI.

MYSTERY VII.—THE HAIR BRACELET.

"My dear Abbé," said Alliette, "I have the greatest esteem for yourself, and the greatest veneration for Cazotte. I admit indubitably the influence exercised by your evil spirits; but allow me to tell you that there is one thing you have forgotten—of which I am a living exemplar. It is this: Death cannot kill the principle of Life: death is but the transformation of the human body into another form; death kills the memory only—that fact, above all. If memory did not die, we should be able to recollect all the peregrinations and transmutations we have undergone, from the beginning of the world until the present moment. The philosopher's stone is but another name for this grand secret; it is the great secret which was discovered by Pythagoras; which was recovered again by St. Germain and Cagliostro; it is now in my possession; and though my body may die, I shall still retain my memory—as I still preserve the recollection of the last four or five centuries: in fact, when I say my body shall die, I am wrong, for there is a body which cannot die—and that is mine."

"Monsieur Alliette," said the doctor, "will you give me permission, beforehand?"

"To do what?"

"To open your grave three months after your decease."

"In one—two—or three months—or years—whenever you please, doctor: only be careful;

for the damage you may cause to my present body may be borne by me in my next form."

"And you believe in this folly?"

"I can give good reasons for my belief. I have been an eye-witness."

"You say you have seen one of those dead-alives?"

"Yes."

"Then, M. Alliette, as every one else has told his tale, you cannot refrain from adding yours to the budget: it would be a curiosity if yours should turn out the most probable of the whole series."

"Probable or no—you shall have the truth. To proceed:—

I was going from Strasbourg to the baths at Louesche. You know the road, doctor?"

"No: but that does not matter. Go on."

Well, I was about to go to the baths at Louesche, from Strasbourg; and, of course, my journey led me to Basle, where I had to leave the public vehicle, and hire a *voiturine*. On my arrival at the Crown hotel, I accordingly made inquiries of the landlord if he knew of any persons going to the baths, who would be willing to share in the expenses of the vehicle, and so make the journey more agreeable and less costly. At night the innkeeper informed me that he had succeeded in procuring a fellow traveller—the wife of a merchant of Basle, who, after scarcely a year's marriage, had lost her child, which she had herself nursed; grief and the change had brought her into a state of ill health for which the waters at Louesche had been recommended. My host further informed me that it was with the greatest reluctance she had consented to part from her husband, whose business forbade him to leave Basle: but that he had prevailed on her, for her health sake, to go, accompanied by her female domestic. I should also add, that a priest, a curate of some little adjoining village, made up our party of four. I could not help remarking, with others, the affection—almost frantic—which seemed to pervade their parting embraces, which lasted during the whole of their way from their room in the hotel to the vehicle in the street. Some even went so far as to remark, that one would think she was going to the Antipodes instead of a journey of 150 miles.

The husband, whose sorrow was scarcely as tumultuous as that of his wife, was, however more moved than, to a common observer, the occasion warranted. However, the parting was effected at last; and giving the ladies the back seat in the vehicle, we set out on our journey. Taking the route to Soleure, the first night we slept at Mundischwyll. Throughout the day, the poor sick woman was uneasy, agitated: at one time, seeing a return vehicle pass us on its way to Basle, it required all the persuasions of her servant to hinder her from returning to her home. On the second day, when near Soleure, on a sudden the lady cried out to the driver to stop, for there was some one pursuing them. I put my head out at the window—the road was perfectly clear—not a man, horse, or vehicle, was in sight.

"You must have been mistaken, madam," said I, "there is nothing on the road besides ourselves."

Page 59.

"It is very strange," she answered, "I am sure I heard a horse galloping behind us;" and as if unwilling to relinquish the idea, she put her head forth and scanned the road narrowly.

"I was mistaken," she said, with a sigh, as she threw herself back into her seat: then she shut her eyes, as if to concentrate her thoughts within herself.

On the third day we had a long stage, for the driver intended to push on for Berne. Just at the same hour as on the preceding evening, the lady, starting from an uneasy slumber, cried out to them to stop, for that she was sure some one was on horseback behind us.

"You are again mistaken, madam," said the coachman, with a smile. "There is no one on the road that I can see on horseback—indeed I can only see three labouring men, who are walking quietly on the road a mile in front of us."

"But I distinctly heard the sound of a horse's feet."

I looked out again, for the tone of the lady's asseveration was so confident as almost to carry conviction with it—the road, with tne exception of the labourers in advance of us, was perfectly free from any appearance of travellers.

"Really, madam," said I, "I must, indeed, tell you, you are deceiving yourself."

"How can I be deceiving myself," she cried, rising, and pointing with her extended hand, "look there! is not that the shadow of a man on horseback.?"

I looked in the direction in which she pointed, and I saw plainly the shadow of a man on horseback and going at a swift pace. But it was in vain that I looked for the real bodies of which the shadows were so plain. I pointed out this remarkable phenomenon to the priest who sat by my side: he said nothing, but very quietly crossed himself.

Gradually the shadows became less distinct, and finally paled away.

Owing to the mental inquietude of the poor lady, the bodily illness she was labouring under became much aggravated before we reached Thun; and she was obliged to travel from thence to Louesche in a litter. Shortly after her arrival, erysipelas developed itself, and for more than a month she was deaf and blind.

But very far from being false was the presentiment that had so weighed on the nervous system of the unhappy wife. She had not gone five leagues from her home, when as we learnt afterwards, her husband had been taken ill at Basle with an inflammation of the brain. The disease made such progress, that on the same day he had taken advantage of a quiet interval to write to his wife, and send it express by a man on horseback. Between Lauffen and Breittenbach, his horse threw the courier headlong on to the road, and his head coming in contact with a stone, his skull had been fractured; he was conveyed to a roadside inn, in a state which rendered him quite incapable of communicating the purport of his errand to any one. Failing the first messenger's return, they had sent another; the same fatality seemed to attach itself to the second as to the first courier, for, having left his horse at the end of the Kander Thal, he had taken a guide to scale the plateau of Schwalbach, which separates the Oberland from Valais; when about half way he was overwhelmed by an avalanche from Mount Attels—the guide narrowly escaping with his life to tell the sad tale.

All this time the malady was making fearful progress. They had been obliged to shave his head, in order to apply ice to the burning brain of the sufferer. From this moment the dying man lost all hope, and, in a moment of relief from delirium, just previous to his death, he wrote the following note:—

"Dear Bertha,

"I am dying; still I would not separate from thee altogether. Promise me that thou wilt save a bracelet made from the hair which they have cut from my head: I will keep some also to be buried with me. Wear it always on thy arm: it seems to me that thus we may still be united.

Thy Frederick."

A third courier started with the message the moment he expired. More fortunate than his predecessors, he reached his destination in safety, and towards the end of the fifth day he arrived at Louesche, at which place he found the lady in the state I have described. It was fully a month after his arrival before the lady recovered her sight and hearing; and another month elapsed ere it was considered prudent to inform her of the death of her husband. Finding her health somewhat re-established, she determined on returning to Basle: and as my rheumatism had disappeared, and I was tired of the place, as well as from feeling an interest in the unhappy woman with whose misfortunes I had thus become acquainted, I proffered her my company to Balse; this she immediately and joyfully accepted; she felt that I was one with she could converse on the only topic dear to her —her husband.

It was a melancholy sight to view the entry of this poor bereaved widow into her widowed home. Living alone as they had, and having no relatives in Basle, the shop had been shut—the place deserted—in fact, with the death of the poor man the whole commercial proceedings of his house had terminated, as a clock when the pendulum is suddenly arrested in its vibrations. They sought the doctor who had attended him in his last moments, and by these means they in some sort resuscitated the sorrows—they reconstructed, as it were, a death which had wellnigh been forgotten by the indifferent world. The poor woman asked for the hair which her husband had bequeathed her. The doctor recollected very well that he had ordered the hair to be taken off; the barber had an equally distinct recollection that he had cut the hair off, but no clue could be obtained as to what had become of it: it was lost, scattered to the winds.

The widowed woman was in despair; the one and only dying wish of her beloved husband thus became a thing incapable of realization. Day after day, and night after night she wandered, more like a shadow than a living woman, about the deserted house. If she attempted to seek a respite from her sorrows in sleep, she was rendered more wretched by dreams of a character which tended to a still greater depression of spirits. These dreams were always followed by a sensation of numbness in the wrist, gradually extending to the heart, and becoming more and more acute, until, as if the agony could no more be borne, even in sleep, she awoke in a state of feverish anxiety and trepidation. In describing the peculiar sensation, she spoke of the pain as if a red-hot iron bracelet had been tightly clasped to her wrist. It was thus quite evident that the preoccupation of the poor woman's mind on the one subject of her husband's dying request weighed heavily and with a fatal influence on her health. She was herself convinced of this, and, with the view of arresting this mental malady, which was fast bringing her to the verge of the grave, she was resolved to have the grave opened and the corpse exhumed, in order, if possible, in some sort to fulfil the last wishes of the defunct.

But here arose an unexpected obstacle: the gravedigger who had officiated at the interment of the husband of the heart-sick woman, had had the last offices of humanity performed for him by another—in short, he had joined the vast crowd for which he had prepared their last resting-place: hence all clue to the particular grave sought for was lost; the newly appointed gravedigger had not the remotest idea of anything connected with the event, and the whole affair of the funeral having been conducted by strangers, no source could be found from whence to derive the desired information.

Still, hoping against hope, the poor woman would repair to the graveyard, throwing eager and anxious glances at the mounds which arose on all sides, and, save in the newly disturbed ground, alike undistinguishable—alike covered by one mass of rank grass and coarse weeds. It was while thus employed, and internally evoking a prayer for assistance and guidance in her research, she fancied she saw the figure of death which was sculptured in relief on one of the tombs near her slowly raise its bony arm, and, with extended finger-bone, point to a corner of the cemetery.

To proceed to the spot, to place a mark on it, was the work of a moment; as she involuntarily turned her gaze towards the grim sculpture, to her astonishment she perceived the hand slowly return to its usual position.

The grave-digger was immediately summoned, and, as I was almost her only friend in the place, I hastened with her to the grave-yard. Though with no very distinct apprehension of the reality of her statement, I yet could not refrain from comparing them with the train of foregone circumstances, and I called vividly to mind the apparition of the man on horseback—the nightly bracelet, with all its attendant horrors—and I could scarcely reconcile my own feelings to anything but a state of nervous excitement.

The grave was opened, the coffin lifted from its bed, and the lid raised. What was our astonishment on finding that not only was the poor woman able to recognise the remains of her departed husband in the corpse before her, but that the hair of the head had so miraculously grown that it had completely covered the shoulders of the corpse. The poor woman knelt by the side of her husband's corpse, and, kissing his brow, detached with a scissors a sufficient quantity of the grave-grown hair for the purpose required.

From the moment the bracelet made from this hair had encircled the wrist of the bereaved widow, the heavy numbing sensation in the wrist was felt no more—: but she afterwards averred that in every moment of anxiety, in every time of threatened danger, she felt a loving pressure—a faint embrace, as it were, from the bracelet on her arm.

"Well my friends, do you believe that the man was really dead. For myself, I cannot believe it."

"Did you hear," said the pale lady, in a voice so singular that its tones sent a thrill through every one in the room, "did you hear anyone say that this corpse was one of those which leave their graves; did you not hear of some one suffering injury from contact with it?"

"I did not," said Alliette, "for I left the country soon after the occurrence."

"Ah!" said the doctor, "you were wrong, M. Alliette, "to quit the scene so soon. Here is Madame Gregoriska, waiting anxiously to make a Polish, Wallachian, or Hungarian vampire of your unfortunate poor Swiss merchant. May I ask, madam," continued he, "if, during your sojourn in the Carpathian mountains, you ever, by chance, encountered any of these vampires?"

"Listen!" said the lady, in a strange, solemn voice: "since every one here has told his story, I also will recount one. I am sure, doctor, you will not dispute the truth of the narrative, for it relates to myself. You will thus know the reason of my being so pallid."

As she spoke, a ray of moonlight streamed through the window, and glancing on the curtain over the couch on which the lady was reclining, threw an unearthly blue tinge on her features, which endowed her with the semblance of a marble statue.

Not a voice welcomed the offer; but the profound silence which reigned around evidenced the anxiety with which all prepared to listen to the tale.

THE LAST MYSTERY.

The Vampire of the Carpathian Mountains.

I am by birth a Pole; my native place being at Sandomir—a country where traditionary legends become articles of faith, where we believe more implicitly in our family traditions than even perhaps in the miracles recorded in Holy Writ. There is not a castle in that country which has not its peculiar spectre;—not a cottage which has not its own familiar sprite.—In the castle, in the cottage—with the rich and the poor—there exists a determined foe and a devoted friend. Sometimes, there is a struggle between these two attendant principles, and a fearful combat for ascendancy.

Such events are accompanied by mysterious noises in the corridors, by hollow roarings amid the turrets of the old towers, tremblings and violent shocks, which cause the inhabitants of castle or cottage to fly from their habitations and seek for aid in the churches, under the shelter of the holy cross and sacred relics, believed to be of peculiar efficacy in such circumstances.

But there is, also, gentlemen, a demon in that unhappy land far more vindictive, more bloody, and more barbarous, it is the demon tyranny, which, in the shape of Russian domination and barbarism, maintains its ascendancy over the bright spirit of liberty, which, though vanquished often, never dies.

The year 1825 saw one of those energetic and deadly struggles—one in which we might imagine that the whole blood of a heroic nation was poured out, and that it had ceased to exist purely from having exhausted its human powers in the dire conflict.

My father and two brothers ranged themselves under the banner of Polish independence —that flag so often struck down—but destined again, I trust, to float in freedom over my unhappy countrymen.

It was in this dire struggle that I lost my two brothers, killed in battle. And a few days after this mournful intelligence reached me— days during which the noise of the heavy cannonading perpetually assailed my ears, and reminded me of the desolation which had stricken our family, I saw my father arrive at our home, with a hundred horsemen, the sole remnant of three thousand men whom he had led to the field. He had returned to his castle, with the intention of defending it to the last extremity, or burying himself in its ruins.

Though, for himself, my father feared not, yet he was tremblingly alive to the horrors which threatened me. He had a life to lose, he knew, for he was resolved never to fall alive into his enemy's hands: but for me there awaited slavery and dishonour—evils far worse than death.

From among the hundred devoted companions-in-arms, he chose twelve; then, calling his steward, he remitted into his hands all the gold and jewels in his possession, and calling to mind that my mother had, previously to the second division of Poland, and under almost similar circumstances, found a refuge in the monastery of Sahastru, situated in the midst of the Carpathian mountains, he ordered him to convey me to that place of security.

Notwithstanding the great affection which my father had ever entertained for me, no great time was consumed in our final adieus. In all human probability, our home would be surrounded by the Russians in less than twenty-four hours: there was, therefore, little time to lose. Dressed in my riding costume, I mounted the surest and best horse in our stables, my father slid his own pistols into the holsters, gave me one last embrace, and the order to set out. During that night and the day following we rode sixty miles, following the course of one of those nameless rivers which empty themselves into the Vistula. Having achieved this, we considered ourselves free from any danger of being taken by the Russians in the rear. The setting sun now

The Fight.

thréw its glorious tints o'er the snowy heights of the Carpathian mountains; on the following day, we had reached their base, and the morning of the third day found us threading our way through one of the mountain gorges.

Far different in their aspect and general features are the Carpathian Mountains from the comparatively tame pictures presented us by the western eminences. In the former we have before our astonished gaze all that can be imagined of the wild, the stern, and the majestic. The stormy summits of those mountains, covered with eternal snow, are lost to our view in the clouds; their sides covered with immense pine forests, throwing their dark shadows over vast lakes resembling seas—those lakes, never ruffled by the dip of oar or the cast of a net, of a depth and stillness and

intensity of blue rivalling the heavens which they so placidly reflect;—the human voice may sometimes be heard in these solitudes chanting some wild Moldavian song, answered by the howl of some lonely wolf or the short bark of the fox—howl, bark, and song being alike repeated in a thousand echoes—as if in astonishment at the audacity which would thus seek to break the grim silence of this dreary world of hills, gorges, valleys, glaciers, lakes, and pine forests. For miles we travelled under the arching shade of the trees, every step revealing some new feature of beauty or grandeur—every turn striking us with astonishment and awe. Here amid these solitudes and the eternal rocks are dangers everywhere: and these dangers of a thousand different aspects: but happily, amidst the whirl of alternate thoughts of admiration, of sur-

The Bandit and his Prize.

prise, of awe, fear has no room to enter in the heart—the sublimity of the danger has neutralized its effect on the nervous system. Sometimes our little path would be crossed by a swift rushing cataract, diverted from its usual course by the fall of an avalanche ; sometimes an immense tree, undermined by the falling soil and continual shifting of the strata, would fall with a deafening crash, bringing a huge mountain of debris of earth, rocks, trees, and bushes across the devious mountain path we were pursuing ; at another time the short but terrific mountain hurricane would sweep our path with its fierce blast, enveloping all round with thick, heavy, driving mists, relieved only by the flashing of forked lightning rending the darkness, and darting hither and thither like a fiery serpent.

Then, after surmounting these Alpine peaks—after traversing these primitive forests,—we find ourselves in a vast endless plain or steppe—a sea without its winds or tempests, a huge savannah, arid and devoid of a trace of vegetation, where the eye looks round in vain for something to break the monotony of the scene ; here the sensation produced is totally different from that of fear—you are overwhelmed by sadness—a vast and profound melancholy, which nothing can distract, for the aspect of the scene around is ever the same ; we ascend and descend a hundred acclivities and declivities, but find ever the same eternal barrenness ; in vain do we look for the traces of a path.   We feel ourselves as if lost in the profundity of our isolation ; in the midst of these deserts, we believe ourselves to be the sole beings in nature; and our melancholy is the abandonment of desolation: in fact, we pursue our way heedless and uncaring, for our journey seems to be for no end—our exertions produce no result: we encounter nor village, nor castle, nor cottage, nor trace of human habitation; here and there, indeed, in the course of this gloomy travel, our route is barred by a little lake, sleeping at the foot of a ravine—neither reed nor bush enliven its dreary banks, but there it lies, like a miniature Dead Sea, staring at us with its dull green eyes; on approaching its sluggish waters, our ears are assailed by the harsh and discordant cry of some aquatic bird, as it slowly rises, and, lazily flapping its wings, flies heavily across the surface of the water. We are obliged to make a detour—we go round this sluggish, waveless lake, we ascend the hillock before us, we descend into another dreary valley, another hillock, another valley, until we seem lost and bewildered, shut up in the midst of an eternal labyrinth of monotony and gloom.

But, passing this chain of alternate forest and steppe, and taking a quick turn towards the south, the view became more grand and less gloomy. We perceive another chain of mountains, more elevated, more picturesque in their outline, more rich in their ever-varying play of light and shadow, clothed with trees to their very summit, and intersected by many a sparkling rivulet and rushing stream; we hear the hermitage bell; we see a party of travellers with waggons slowly winding along the serpentine path on the side of an adjacent mountain, and, by the last rays of the setting sun, we perceive, hidden nestling among the hills, like a covey of frightened birds, the white cottages of a village, huddled close together, as if to form a defence against some nocturnal surprise: for with life and society come danger—not, as was the case in the savage fastnesses we have before described—that danger is to be feared from the attack of hungry bear or savage wolf—but from hordes of far more savage brigands.

However, we kept on our way: ten days' travel had we accomplished, and not the trace of an accident. We could already perceive the hoary top of Mount Pion, towering above the heads of the neighbouring mountains,—like the eldest born among a family of giants—and, on an overhanging cliff on its southern side we could discern the convent of Sahastru, to which we were bound. Three days more, and we should be there.

It was now the end of July: our journey had been under a burning sun, and it was with a feeling of voluptuous pleasure that, as night came on, we inhaled the cool mountain breeze. We had passed the tower and ruins of Niantzo. We then descended into a plain, that we now saw led towards an opening into the mountains; from this spot we could trace the course of the Britza, its banks enamelled with the bright red bloom of the geranium and the white flower of the great campanula. We next traversed the side of a precipice, at the foot of which rolled the river,—which, even at this time of the year, was almost a torrent; here the path was so narrow that it was with difficulty we could go two abreast.

Our guide led the way, lazily lying on his side, and chanting, in a monotonous tone, a wild Morlaque song, the words of which I followed with an interest I could not account for. The singer was his own poet; as for the air, it must be given by one of those mountaineers in order to render it with all its wild melancholy —its native simplicity. As near as I can recollect, these are the words:

In Savila's morass there lieth a corpse;
    No son of Illyria—but brigand is he:
A ball through his heart—a sword through his throat,
    Revenge the foul wrong he had done to Marie.

But stranger than all, though three days have passed,
    Since the heart of the brigand hath ceased to beat,
The blood from his death-wound hath ceased not to well
    And water the roots of the pine at its feet.

Fly then, poor traveller, the light of that eye,
    Though life in its brightest effulgence may gleam;
E'en the wolf, although starving, averts his gaunt eyes,
    And the vulture flies from it—though corse it may seem.

'Tis the vampire within that makes the blood flow,
    'Tis the fiend's burning glance that illumines that eye;
Oh! touch not that corpse—'tis the vampire's own dwelling,
    And whoso that touches the dread one shall die.

Scarcely had the man finished his low chant when the sound of firearms and the whistling of bullets were heard. Our guide, mortally wounded, fell from his horse and rolled to the bottom of the precipice: the animal, trembling with terror, stood stretching his head over the abyss wherein his master had disappeared. At the same moment loud cries were heard, and we saw, posted on the sides of the opposite mountain, about thirty bandits: we were completely surrounded. Each one of our little party seized his arms, and, being all old soldiers, and no ways intimidated by the smell of gunpowder, prepared to repel the attack. For myself, taking my pistols from the holsters, and, seeing at a glance the disadvantages of our present position, I gave my horse the spur, shouted "Forward!" and pushed for the plain.

But we had to deal with mountaineers;—men who bounded from rock to rock, like real demons of the abyss, aiming and firing as they jumped, and keeping always on our flank the advantageous position they had at first taken. Another misfortune was, that our manœuvre had been foreseen by our enemies. At the end of a narrow gorge, where the road became wider, and the mountain opened out into a terrace, a young man was stationed with a force of ten or twelve cavaliers. On perceiving us, they put their steeds to the gallop, and dashed on towards our little troop, while those who pursued us in the rear scattered themselves on our flank, and thus we were environed by foes on all sides. Our situation now began to assume a serious aspect; meanwhile, habituated from infancy to hear and witness scenes of war and bloodshed, I looked at my position, and lost no particle of what was passing around.

Each of our assailants, clothed in sheep-skins, wore a large, round hat, crowned with wild flowers, like the Hungarians, and each carried in his hand a long Turkish musket, which they shook in the air after firing, uttering savage cries of defiance and exultation; to the girdle was attached a curved sabre and a pair of pistols.

Their chief was a young man of about two-and-twenty years of age, of pale complexion, with large, black eyes, and his long hair hanging on his shoulders. His costume was composed of a Moldavian robe, encircled with fur, and slashed in the sleeve, with bands of gold and silk. A curved sabre was in his hand, while four pistols were in his girdle. During the firing he continually poured forth harsh and inarticulate cries, which to me seemed to appertain to no human language, but which, however, had the effect of explaining his wishes; for the men under his command implicitly obeyed their tenor—sometimes falling on the ground to avoid our fire—rising again to return it,—knocking down those who were standing on their legs, and despatching those who were lying wounded—so that the affair was, on their side, a complete butchery. One after another, I had seen eight of the twelve of my brave defenders put to death. The remainder surrounded me, and, knowing that they had no mercy to expect, only desired to sell their lives as dearly as they could.

A more expressive cry—harsher, shriller, and more barbarous,—was uttered by the young chief, at the same time he held the point of his sabre towards us. I had no doubt as to the meaning of this order—it was to give us the finishing stroke, for every man brought his musket to the level: I felt that my last hour was come. Uttering a short prayer, and raising my eyes to heaven, I awaited death. As I raised my eyes I saw, not descending, but throwing himself, as it were, over the intervening rocks, a young man, who, taking his stand upon a stone which overlooked the scene, like a statue on a pedestal, extended his hands towards the scene of carnage, and in a loud voice uttered one word "Stop!" At the sound of his voice, every eye was lifted towards him, every musket was lowered—all seemed to obey this new master, except one, who again put his gun to his shoulder and fired. The ball broke the arm of one of my surviving friends: and the bandit who had fired his piece spurred his horse to put a period to the wounded man's existence. He had not gone four-yards from his starting place ere he fell from his horse, a dead man—shot through the head by the new-comer. Until this moment I had kept up my strength and resolution: but the reaction overpowered me, and I fainted. When I recovered my senses, I found myself on the grass, my head resting on the knees of a young man, of whom I could see nothing but a white hand, which encircled my waist,—whilst standing before me, his arms crossed, and his sabre tucked under his arm, stood the young Moldavian chief who had directed the attack.

"Kostaki," said the young man in French, and in a tone of authority which helped much to sustain my hopes, "you will instantly withdraw your men, and leave to me the care of this lady."

"Brother — brother," answered the young man to whom these words were addressed, and who seemed hardly capable of restraining his wrath, "brother, take care you do not weary my patience. I have left the castle to you, leave the forest to me. At the castle, you are the master; in the forest, I will reign supreme. Here, I have only to say one word, and I force you to obey me."

"Kostaki, I am the eldest—that is to say, I am master—in the forest as in the chateau—here as well as there. Oh! I am like yourself, of the blood of Brankovan—royal blood flows in my veins; I have the right to command, and I will be obeyed."

"You may command your valets, but you shall not interfere with my soldiers."

"Soldiers they are not: brigands they are—brigands whom I will hang at our turret windows, if they hesitate one moment to obey me."

"Very good: you had better try that with their commander."

The young man withdrew his support, and placed me gently on the ground. I looked at him for a moment, and I saw at a glance that this was he who had fallen, as it were, from heaven, in the midst of our foes. He was a young man of about four-and-twenty; tall and commanding in mien, graceful and handsome in person and contenance, with large blue eyes, in which could be discovered a singular mixture of resolution and tenderness. His long, fair hair, which bespoke his Sclavonian race, fell in wavy ringlets over his shoulders; a disdainful smile hung on his lips,—disclosing a row of pearly white teeth; his whole aspect had the *fierté*, the resolution, and the proud bearing which might be attributed to the archangel Michael, when combatting the power of the Evil One. He was dressed in a velvet tunic; a small bonnet, such as we often see in the pictures by Raphael, adorned with a simple eagle's feather, covered his head. His waist was encircled by a girdle, supporting a hunting sword: in one hand he carried a small double-barrelled carbine,—of the accuracy of the aim from one of the barrels there was ample witness in the bandit who lay dead by his side.

He extended his hand with a commanding gesture, which even the bandit chief seemed involuntarily to obey, and addressed a few words in the Moldavian language to the bandits. This seemed to make a profound impression upon them. Their chief then, in the same language, addressed his followers in a somewhat long speech, accompanied, as I could judge from his manner, by many imprecations and menaces. To this my deliverer made no reply; and his followers merely bowed their heads in silence.

The elder brother now made a gesture, and the bandits immediately ranged themselves on our side.

"Be it so, Gregoriska," said Kostaki, again using the French language. "This lady shall not be taken to the cavern: but still she belongs to me. I found her, fought for her fairly, and will have her."

So saying, he threw himself to the ground, and lifted me in his arms.

"The lady shall be conducted to the castle, and put under the care of my mother; and I will not quit her until that is done," replied my protector.

"My horse!" cried Kostaki, in Moldavian.

Castle of Brankovan.

This order was obeyed. Gregoriska looked round, and seizing by the bridle a horse which had lost its master, vaulted into the saddle without touching the stirrups.

Kostaki lost no time in following the example of his brother, still holding me in his arms, and immediately put his horse into a gallop. The horse of Gregoriska seemed at the same moment to have received the same impulsion—it was a neck and neck race.

It was indeed a strange sight to see these two horsemen riding side by side—sombre, silent—neither losing sight of one another for an instant, but, without seeming to interfere with one another; apparently abandoning themselves to the guidance of their horses, they bounded over rocks, through woods, by precipices. My head being turned over my captor's shoulder, I could see the clear blue eyes of Gregoriska fixed upon my own. Kostaki soon perceived this, and instantly shifted my head, and I could see nothing more than the sombre yet flashing glance of him who held me in his arms. I lowered my eyelids, it was in vain; the quick, lightning flash of his ardent, burning gaze, seemed to penetrate to the inmost depths of my soul. It was then a strange sensation came over me; methought I was, like Lenora in the ballad of Burger, carried away by phantom horsemen; and it was not without a sensation of terror that I opened my eyes when our speed was arrested, almost expecting to see myself surrounded by broken crosses and desecrated tombs.

We entered the courtyard of a Moldavian castle, built in the fourteenth century.

Gregoriska.

CHAPTER XII.

THE CHATEAU OF BRANKOVAN.

QUICK as lightning Kostaki let me glide from his arms to the ground, and as quickly he stood by my side: but quick as he was, his movements were followed as rapidly by Gregoriska. We were received by the domestics; and it was quite evident, though every attention was paid to Kostaki, that his brother was the master. Giving an order to a female, he made a sign for me to follow her. There was so much of true respect in the look which accompanied this sign, that I did not hesitate for one moment. Five minutes after I found myself in a chamber, which, bare and uninhabitable as it would appear to any one the least

fastidious as to appearances, was evidently the best furnished room in the castle.

It was a large square apartment, with a sort of raised divan of green serge, forming a seat in the day, a bed at night; five or six great, lumbering oak chairs, a large chest, and, in one of the angles, a dais, something like a grand cathedral stall. As for the curtains, those for the window answered a similar purpose for the bed. We ascended into this chamber by a flight of steep stairs, on which were three colossal statues of Brankovan.

Scarcely had I had time to make a few necessary changes in my toilette, which the long journey and its events had rendered necessary, when a low knock at the door struck my ear.

"Come in," said I, of course in French—by the way, you know that the French language is spoken almost universally by the Polish nation. Gregoriska entered.

"Ah, madam," said he, "I am so happy to find that you speak French."

"And I also, sir," I answered, "am happy to speak it, because I can, thanks to this accident, appreciate your generous conduct towards me. It is in this language you have befriended me against the design of your brother—it is in this language that I offer you my sincere thanks."

"I have simply done an act of duty towards a lady, circumstanced as you were. I had been hunting in the mountains when I heard the irregular discharge of fire-arms. I had heard that an attack of the Russian army had been expected: thinking this was its beginning, I marched briskly to the field, to use a military phrase. Thank God! I arrived in good time. But allow me to ask, madam, by what accident a lady of distinction like yourself has ventured to trust herself in our mountains?"

"I am a native of Poland, sir," I answered, "my two brothers were killed in the Russian war, my father, whom I left preparing to defend his house against the barbarians, has, ere this, no doubt joined his sons in another world, and I, by his orders, have come to seek a refuge in the monastery of Sahastru, where my mother, in her youth and under similar circumstances, sought and found a safe asylum."

"You are an enemy to Russia: so much the better, my dear madam," said the young man; "this title will prove to you a powerful auxiliary in this castle; and believe me you will have need of all that can aid you in the forthcoming struggle. Now, madam, that I know who you are, let me inform you who we are. The name of Brankovan, perhaps, may not be strange to you?"

I bowed.

"My mother is the last princess of that name —the last descendant of that illustrious chief who put to death Cantimir, the infamous favourite of Peter I. My mother married, firstly, Serban Waiwode,—head of a princely house, but of less renown. My father had been educated at Vienna; and could therefore well appreciate the advantages of civilization. He resolved that I should partake of the same privileges — that I should have a European education; and with that end we started for France, Italy, Germany, and Spain.

"My mother (it is not, I know well, for a son to speak of a mother that which I am about to tell you, but there are circumstances which render strange things necessary—and I hope this will be a sufficient excuse for the revelation I am about to make.) My mother, during the first travels of my father, formed a criminal connexion with one of the leaders of a band of men whom we call partisans—such as those who attacked your party to-day: this man, Count Giordaki Koproli,—half Greek, half Moldavian —wrote to my father, informing him of all the circumstances, and demanding a divorce; resting this demand upon the fact that my mother, a Brankovan, was the wife of a man who was making himself, day by day, a greater stranger to his country. Alas! my father could not consent to this, which may appear strange, when we consider, that, among ourselves, such a course is a thing

of common and constant occurrence. However, my father shortly after died of an aneurism, and the letter fell into my hands. I had no wish on the subject, save that I had a sincere desire that my mother should be happy. With this view, I immediately forwarded a letter to her, informing her that she was a widow: in the same letter I asked for permission to continue my travels. I had determined I would never meet at my father's house a man whom I detested—the husband of my mother; for I need not tell you that she gave that title to her *ci-devant* lover: and I was about to take up my fixed residence in France, when I was informed that Count Giordaki Koproli had been assassinated by some of my father's Cossack tenantry.

"I hastened home. I ever fondly loved my mother; I knew her isolation, and the void she would experience in her heart, which nothing but the love of a child could so well supply. Though she had never shewn towards me any excess of maternal affection, yet was I her son.

"I entered the home of my fathers, unannounced, unattended, unexpected. I found there a young man, whom I supposed to be a stranger, but I soon discovered him to be my mother's son.

"It was Kostaki—the child of adultery,—but legitimatised by a second marriage; it was Kostaki, the untameable, brutal being that you have seen, whose passions are his sole law, who regards nothing as sacred in this world save his mother, whom he obeys as the tiger, which, while crouching under the hand of his keeper, never fails to growl its ineffectual rage, never loses the hope that some time or other it shall be revenged. In the interior of this castle, in the house of Brankovan and Waiwode, I am still master; but once outside that boundary—once in the fields, Kostaki becomes the savage child of the woods and the mountains, who would make all things living bow to his iron will. How he conceded yesterday; how it was that his men gave up their butchery, I know not—perhaps from old habits, or some lingering relics of the respect they owe to my name. But I would not dare to run such another risk. If you remain here—if you quit not this chamber, this court, nor go outside those walls, I can answer for your safety. Make but one step beyond the threshold of this castle, and I answer for nothing but this, my life shall be devoted to defending you."

"But why cannot I, in accordance with my father's wishes, continue my route towards the convent of Sahastru?"

"Do it—try it—give your orders—I will accompany you. For myself, I shall be found on the road; you—you—I cannot tell you; but you will never reach the convent."

"What, then, can I do?"

"Remain here: wait—take counsel of events and profit by circumstances. Fancy that you are fallen into a nest of bandits, that your courage can alone help you out of the dilemma; that your coolness and resolution are your only chances of safety. My mother, in spite of her preference for Kostaki, the son of her love, is noble and generous. She is a Brankovan, and a true princess. You shall see her. She will defend you from the brutality of Kostaki. Put yourself under her protection: she will undoubtedly love you—for—(and here he looked at me with an indefinable expression of tenderness and respect)—no one can see you and not love you. Come now to the supper-room, where my mother awaits you. Do not shew either embarassment or defiance; speak in the Polish language—no one here knows it beside myself; I will translate what you say to my mother—and you may rest satisfied that I shall be your faithful interpreter. But, above all, say not a word of what I have revealed to you in confidence. Come."

I followed him down the stairs, which were lighted by pine torches stuck into iron hands protruding from the wall; and it was evident to me that this was an illumination quite unusual, and only made on my account. On arriving at the dining-room, Gregoriska opened the door, and pronouncing the words "*The Stranger*" in Moldavian, a tall lady advanced to meet me. It was the Princess Brankovan. Her grey hair was plaited around her head, which was covered by a turban, surmounted by a tuft of feathers—emblem of her princely origin. She wore a tunic of golden tissue, and her corsage, strewn with precious stones, was covered by a long robe of Turkish manufacture, edged with fur. In her hands she carried a chaplet of amber beads, which she unceasingly and with a quick spasmodic action rolled between her fingers.

By the side of his mother stood Kostaki, clad in a splendid Magyar costume, which made him in my eyes more remarkable still. It consisted of a loose large-sleeved robe of green velvet, falling below his knees: his pantaloons were of red cachmere; and his slippers of Turkish morocco, embroidered with gold. His head was bare, and his long hair, almost of a blue black, fell in heavy masses on his bare neck, round which was only seen the slight edging of a silk under-vest. He saluted me with some traces of confusion in his manner, and spoke a few words which were to me unintelligible.

"You speak French, brother," said Gregoriska; "the lady is a Pole, and understands that language."

Kostaki pronounced a few common-place words; his French was nearly as unintelligible to me as was his Moldavian; but his mother, taking him by the arm, interrupted him. Her gestures clearly told me that she informed him that my welcome to the castle ought to proceed, not from Kostaki, but from herself.

Although entirely ignorant of the language in which the lady spoke, I could judge from her manner and the expression of her features that she was giving me a cordial welcome. She then led me to the table, pointed to a seat next her own—indicated the various members of the household, and seating herself with a graceful dignity, crossed herself, and invoked a blessing.

Immediately each one took his seat. Regulated by a strict etiquette, Gregoriska's place was next to mine: this left a vacant place of honour for Kostaki by the side of his mother, Smerande, for such was the name of the Countess. Gregoriska was attired in a costume similar to that of his brother; a magnificent decoration hung on his breast; it was the order of Medjidie of Sultan Mahmoud. Every member of the household sat at the same table: each one placed according to his rank. The supper was a very dolorous affair: once only Kostaki spoke to me: his brother occasionally spoke to me in French; whilst the mother proffered me the civilities of the occasion with a dignified, solemn, stately air—which fully bore out the assertion of Gregoriska, that she was truly a princess.

Immediately after supper, Gregoriska took occasion to represent to his mother that I wished to retire, and how necessary it was that I should repose after the fatigues and incidents of my journey. Smerande made a sign in the affirmative, and taking me by the hand, she kissed my brow, as if I had been her daughter, wishing me a good night. Gregoriska had rightly conjectured. I did indeed long for the privacy of my own chamber. I thanked the princess, who, escorting me to the door, gave me in charge of two female attendants, who led the way to my chamber. It was the same that I had quitted to go to the dining room: the sofa or rather divan had been transferred into a bed: in all other respects it was as I had left it.

Dismissing the two attendants, I stood alone in this vast chamber. Looking round, I saw that besides that by which I entered, there were two other doors in the room: but the immense iron bolts which were drawn across on the inside gave sufficient proof of strength and security. Turning to the door by which I had entered I found that this also was properly secured. On opening the window, I discovered beneath it a precipice. Reassured, I went back to the sofa: on the table near it I found a folded note. I opened it—it was in the Polish language, and to the following purport:

"Sleep in peace : nothing can harm you whilst you remain in the interior of the castle.

"GREGORISKA."

I followed his advice implicitly: for, wearied with the day's excitement, I was soon sound asleep in the Castle of Brankovan.

CHAPTER XIV.

THE TWO BROTHERS.

FROM that moment I became a resident at the castle: and here begins the drama which I am about to narrate.

The two brothers became enamoured of me. Each one shewed the passion, modified by peculiarities of disposition and education. Kostaki made no scruple to inform me that he loved me: swore that I should be his, and no one else's; that he would kill me sooner than that I should be another's, whomsoever he might be. Gregoriska, on the contrary, said nothing; but he overwhelmed me with assiduous care and attention. All the resources which a brilliant education could afford;—all the remembrances of a youth spent in the courts and among the highest ranks of the nobility of Europe—were enlisted for my pleasure and amusement. Alas! it was not difficult for him to please or amuse me: when I first heard his voice, it was like the caressing tones of love to my heart; I felt

"By the side of his mother stood Kostaki, clad in a splendid Magyar costume."—*Page 75.*

the first glance of his eyes penetrate my soul.

Three months had passed, and Kostaki had a thousand times told me that he loved me, and that he knew I hated him. Gregoriska had not spoken to me a word of love: yet I felt that, whenever he thought fit to claim my hand, it was his.

Smerande also loved me passionately—but her love was somewhat fearful. She evidently and openly espoused the cause of Kostaki; and appeared even more jealous of me than her favoured son could be. Not understanding the Polish or French language, and I being in a similar state of ignorance of the Moldavian language, I was spared the infliction of any verbal solicitations on her part: but she had acquired three words of French, which she took a delight in repeating to me, kissing me on the brow as she said—"Kostaki loves Hedwige."

It was now that I received news which seemed the crowning misfortune of my unhappy life. My father—as I heard from one of the men who had been taken prisoner with me, and liberated on condition of his bringing back news of my parents—had died defending his hearth. Our home had been taken, and burnt to the ground: I was alone in the world, without home, friends, or means.

Kostaki now redoubled his persecuting addresses, and his mother her proofs of tenderness; on the pretext that, isolated as I was, I must perforce stand in need of consolation.

Gregoriska had frequently spoken to me of the peculiar faculty with which the Moldavians were endowed of preventing by outward signs

The Two Brothers.

any detection or recognition of their real feelings and opinions. He was himself, a living example of this tenacity of secrecy. No one could be more certain of anything in the world than I was of the fact that I was beloved by him, yet if any one had asked me to specify or detail one proof—one word—one outward and visible sign of that love, I could not have done so: for never had he touched my hand—never had his eyes sought mine. Jealousy alone could then have suggested to Kostaki my love for Gregoriska: love alone could to me have divined that by Gregoriska I was loved. I will confess, in spite of all this, that this impassibility—this impenetrable reserve, caused in me a feeling of uneasiness. I believed, certainly—but it seemed to me as if it was not enough—I longed to hear of his love from his own lips.

One night, as I was about to retire to my couch, I heard some one knock softly at one of the two doors which I have before told you was locked on the inside: from the style of the knocking, I felt convinced it was a friend. I therefore went to the door, and asked who was there.

"Gregoriska," replied a voice, in tones which left me in no doubt as to who was the speaker.

"What do you want?" I asked him, trembling.

"If you have any confidence in me—if you believe me to be a man of honour, grant me one request I am about to make?"

"What is it?"

"Put out your light, as if you had retired to bed, and in half a hour from this open the door to me."

" Come in half an hour," was my only answer."

I extinguished my lamp, and waited in silence and trembling—for the beating of my heart told me something important was about to occur. Slowly the minutes passed : but the half hour elapsed, and the same soft knock I had before heard was repeated. I had pushed back the bolt in the interval, and therefore had but to open the door.

Gregoriska entered, and I fastened the door behind him. He remained a moment silent and motionless, imposing the same by a gesture on myself. Then, having apparently satisfied himself that no danger menaced us, he came into the centre of the vast chamber, and feeling from my trembling that I could scarce stand, he brought me a chair, into which I fell, rather than sat.

"Oh, my God!" said I, "what is the matter—why these precautions—why this visit ?"

"Because my life—but that is nothing—because your life depends on my interview with you this night."

I caught hold of his hand, in a paroxysm of fear. He lifted it to his lips, and then, as if abashed at his audacity, he relinquished it, and looked into my eyes for pardon. My eyes fell beneath his gaze: he could there read no disapproval.

" I love you!" he said to me, in a voice low and sweet as a song-bird's; "do you love me ?"

" I do," I replied.

" Will you consent to be my wife ?"

" Yes."

He put his hand across his brow, with a deep sigh—but a sigh of happiness. "Then you will not refuse to follow me ?"

" I will go with you anywhere."

" For you must know," he continued, " that our only hope of happiness is in flight."

" Yes—yes !" I cried—"let us fly."

" Hush, hush !" he said, " I'll tell you what I have done—what I have been doing all this time that I have loved you, but without avowing it. I hesitated to avow it before, because I wished that, once sure of your love, there should be no bar to our union. I am rich, Hedwige—immensely rich—but I am rich only in the goods which a Moldavian nobleman possesses—I am rich in lands, in flocks, in serfs. Well, I have sold all for a million, to the Monastery of Hango—land, flocks, villagers. They have given me three hundred thousand francs in jewels ; a hundred thousand gold louis d'ors ; and the rest I have in bills drawn upon a banker in Vienna. Is that enough ?"

" Your love is sufficient for me,—is it not, Gregoriska ;" said I, as I took his hand in mine.

" Well, listen. I shall go to-morrow to the Monastery of Hango to make my final arrangements with the Superior. He will keep horses in readiness for us, hidden about a hundred yards from the castle. After supper, you will retire as usual ; you must extinguish your lamp as you have done to-night—and I shall visit you as I have done now. But the next day, instead of my going alone, you must accompany me, we gain the door, reach the fields—find our horses—mount—and the next morning shall find us thirty leagues from this place."

" But shall we not rest after that ?"

" Dear Hedwige !"

Gregoriska pressed me to his heart ; our lips met.

Oh ! it was truly a man of honour to whom I had opened my door ; he knew well that I did not belong to him bodily, though my soul was his.

It was little I slept that night. I pictured myself flying with Gregoriska ; I felt myself borne in his arms as I had previously been in those of Kostaki ; but, instead of a journey horrible and affrighting, dreary and heart-sickening, this picture was of a sweet and ravishing embrace, the bliss of which would be enhanced by the voluptuous velocity of our pace—for there is in swift motion an enjoyment which, when the heart is light, few things can surpass.

However, morning came, and I descended to the rooms below. It struck me that the frown on Kostaki's brow, as he saluted me, was darker than usual. His grim smile had exchanged its ironical usual expression for a malignant and even menacing flash of his dark eyes. His mother's salute was as cordial as usual.

At luncheon, Gregoriska ordered his horses ; Kostaki apparently took no notice of this. About one o'clock, Gregoriska took his leave, begging his mother not to wait dinner for him, as he should not be back before night ; then, turning to me, he begged me to excuse his absence, and went from the room. It was at that moment that I caught a momentary glance of the eye of Kostaki as it fell on his brother's retreating form, and I shuddered at the concentration of malignant, undying hatred which it displayed.

How that day passed I know not ; to me it seemed as if I was in a trance. I had made no confidant of our project : hardly had I, in my prayers, dared to avow it even to my God—yet it seemed to me as if every one knew my secret—every eye that was fixed on me seemed to scan the secret recesses of my heart

The dinner was indeed a terror : dark in his visage, frowning in his features, silent in his manner, Kostaki spoke rarely, he merely addressed himself once or twice, in Moldavian, to his mother—and each time the deep, guttural harshness of his voice made me tremble.

When I arose to retire to my chamber, Smerande, as was her custom, embraced me, and, in so doing, made use of the French phrase, which I had not heard from her lips for some days before.

" Kostaki loves Hedwige !"

I had often heard her repeat this, parrot-like, before, but never had it grated on my feelings as now—it followed me like a threat of evil. Whilst sitting alone in my chamber, it was as if some voice was perpetually hissing into my ears, "Kostaki loves Hedwige !" And the love of Kostaki, I said almost aloud, Gregoriska has told me is death !

It was about seven o'clock, and just as day was declining, that I saw from my window Kostaki cross the court-yard of the castle. He turned himself round, as if to scan my window. I threw myself back into the shade, so as to avoid his gaze. I was extremely uneasy, for, as far as my position would allow me to judge, he was directing his steps towards the stables. In order to assure myself as to this, I hazarded the opening one of the doors which led to the adjoining room, the window of which completely overlooked the stable-yard. It was as I suspected; I saw him take from the stable his own favourite horse, and saddle him with the care of a man who attaches some importance to the minutest detail of his occupation. He was dressed, as when I first saw him, in his mountain costume, and was armed only with his sabre. Having equipped his horse for the road, he again threw a long, piercing glance at the window of my bed-room. His search was unsuccessful, and, with a scowl on his brow, he vaulted into the saddle, and quitted the castle, taking the road to the monastery of Hango.

Oh! the vague presentiment of evil which then shook my soul: my boding heart told me his intention was to waylay his brother.

I remained rooted to the window until a bend in the road shut him out from my phrenzied gaze. Night came on, throwing its thick veil of darkness over everything, and mixing in one undistinguishable shadow, tree, forest, mountain, and turret, yet there I remained.

At last, my impatience and anxiety gave me the strength and energy I had before lacked. My nerves were strung to know the worst. I descended the stairs to the rooms below; here I saw Smerande. The absence of any change in her usual placid habits convinced me she must have been a stranger to anything of importance occurring between her sons; her orders for supper were given as usual, and I saw two covers laid for the brothers.

I could question no one. Besides, how was I to do so, if I wished it? No one in the castle, with the exception of Gregoriska and Kostaki, could speak either of the two languages I was master of. Nine o'clock was the usual hour for supper: at half-past eight I had left my bed-room to come down stairs. During that half hour I remained silent, absorbed in thought, and anxiously following with my eyes the slow movement of the hands of the huge-faced clock which stood in the room. A few minutes before nine I thought I heard the sound of a horse's feet entering the court-yard at a gallop. Smerande heard it also, for she turned her head quickly towards the window, but the night was too dark to see anything outside.

I have said that it was the sound of one horse's feet only that we heard. I knew well that but one of the two horsemen who left that court-yard in the day would ever recross that court-yard at night.

But which of the twain?

Footsteps resounded in the antechamber—footsteps slow and heavy—ah! how heavily they pressed on my heart. A shadow darkened the threshold—I breathed again—it was Gregoriska. One moment more of suspense, and my heart would have broken! I have said I recognised Kostaki—but he was pale as death. No one could have looked on him and not have known that some terrible event had taken place.

"Is it thou, Kostaki?" inquired Smerande.

"No—mother," he replied in a low, hollow tone.

"Ah! you are come," said she, "and since when is it that your mother ought to wait for you?"

"It is not nine o'clock, mother." And, in fact, as he spoke, the clock struck the hour.

"True," said Smerande. "Where is your brother?"

In spite of myself I could not help thinking of the question that God put to Cain.

Gregoriska made no answer.

"Has any one seen Kostaki?" demanded Smerande in an impatient tone.

The *avatar*, or house steward, informed her that, at seven o'clock, the count went to the stables, saddled his horse, and took the Hango road.

At this moment my eyes encountered Gregoriska's. I am not sure whether it was reality or hallucination, but I fancied I saw a drop of blood on his brow. I slowly carried my finger to my own brow, and by so doing indicated to him the spot. Gregoriska comprehended me: he took his handkerchief and wiped his brow.

"Yes—yes," murmured Smerande, "he has probably encountered some bear in the mountains, or some vagabond wolf, which he has amused himself with hunting: and these are things which make a mother wait for a child. Where did you leave him, Gregoriska?" said she.

"I assure you, mother, that my brother did not go out with me," was the answer.

"Very well. Serve, and shut the outer door. Let those that are without sleep without."

The first part of the order was executed to the letter; Smerande took her place at the head of the table, Gregoriska occupied the seat at her right hand—I sat opposite him.

The domestics were about to execute the last order given by the princess, when we heard the noise of a great tumult in the court, and one of the valets, in a state of great consternation, entered the upper room, and said,

"Princess, count Kostaki's horse has just galloped riderless into the court yard; the saddle is stained with blood."

"Ah!" murmured Smerande, with a pale face and fearfully menacing gesture "it was thus with his poor father."

I cast my eyes furtively upon Gregoriska: he was not merely pale, but livid.

Taking a torch from the hand of one of the servitors, Smerande went to the door, opened it, and descended to the court yard, where stood the horse, still affrighted, held by two or three grooms, whose united efforts were required to appease his fretful motions. Smerande went up to the animal, and attentively examined the spots of blood on the saddle.

"Kostaki has met death face to face with his enemy—it was a duel, and he had one adversary only. My children, search for his corpse—afterwards we will seek for his murderer."

Immediately the whole body of serving men rushed out at the door by which the horse had entered: we could see their torches flashing at intervals in the fields and through the dense mass of foliage in the forest, like the meteors in the marshes of Pisa.

" Kostaki has met death face to face with his enemy."—*Page* 79.

Smerande, as if aware that the search would not occupy much time, still stood at the threshold of the door. Not a tear wetted the cheeks of that bereaved mother: though the despair which was in her heart appeared in the dark and gloomy restleness of her eyes. Gregoriska stood a little behind her: I was near him.

After a quarter of an hour of anxiety, we saw the servitors returning,—not separated, as they went forth, but all united in one body—and their torches fitfully gleaming on some dark object which they carried in the centre. Nearer it came: they carried a litter, on it a corpse. Slowly the procession toiled up the steep ascent leading to the entrance of the castle: and having crossed the yard, each uncovered his head, and the dead body was reverently deposited in the hall.

With a gesture of almost sublime dignity, Smerande made signs for the crowd to stand back from the corpse: then, approaching it, she knelt at its side, and putting apart the dark hair which veiled the features, she contemplated the dead in silence for some time—still not a tear escaped those burning eyeballs—not a sob escaped from those rigid bloodless lips. Then, opening the robe which he wore, she discovered the blood-stained linen vest. The wound was in the right breast, and had evidently been caused by a straight two-edged blade: and it immediately brought to my mind the short two-edged bayonet which Gregoriska used to attach to his carbine. I looked to see if he wore it at his side—it was not there. The mother called for water, and bathed the wound, from which slowly trickled a rill of fresh blood.

Smerande exacting an oath from Gregoriska.—*Page* 81.

The spectacle which met the eye at this moment was one as sublime as it was horrible. The vast lofty chamber, half lighted up with the torches, half in dim shadow and obscured with the resinous smoke—the savage men who stood round the corpse, their dark eyes glittering with ferocity, their strange and barbarous costume,—the tearless, despairing mother, calculating, with fixed eye and knitted brow, the time which had elapsed since the death-blow was given to her beloved son—the stern silence, only interrupted now and then by the half-smothered sob of some brigand more than ordinarily attached to his chief, now lying dead before his eyes—all this, I have said, presented at one glance a combination of the horrible and the sublime.

Kissing the pallid brow of her dead child, Smerande arose; and, throwing aside the long plaits of her grey hair which had dropped across her pale face, she called aloud for Gregoriska.

Gregoriska trembled at the voice; then shaking his head, as if to throw off the physical palsy which mental agony had occasioned, he answered.

"Come here, my son, and listen to what I say."

Gregoriska obeyed with a shudder.

As he approached the body, the blood ran fresher and more abundantly from the wound. Happily Smerande was not looking, or she would have needed no farther search for the murderer.

"Gregoriska," said she, "I know too well that Kostaki and you never loved each other. I know well that thou hast a Waiwode for a father, and he a Koproli; but, by the mother of both, who stands before you, ye are both Brankovans. I know thou art a man of the western world, and that he who now lies cold and dead before us was a child of the mountains of the east—still, by that mother who bore you both, ye were brothers. Gregoriska, I ask thee, can we carry my son to lie with his father—could I ever rest —if we neglected—had *I* neglected to exact an oath from thee to revenge his murder—to punish his murderer."

"Name my brother's murderer, madame, and give your orders. I swear to you, if he exists, that before an hour elapses he shall cease to live."

"Swear, Gregoriska, swear to me as follows— swear it, under penalty of a mother's curse. Hear me, my son. Swear that the murderer shall die; that thou wilt not leave one stone of his house standing upon another; that his mother, his children, his brothers, his wife, shall fall by thy hands. Swear—and, in swearing, call upon the wrath of heaven to crush thee if thou failest in one tittle of this thy oath. If thou breakest this oath, then shalt thou be cursed by thy mother and friends, and execrated by the world."

Gregoriska put his hand on the corpse, and said, "I swear that the murderer shall die."

As the words were uttered, I thought the eyes of the dead man rolled in their sockets, and threw a lurid glance of never-dying, burning love towards me, and one of hatred to his brother.

I could support no more—I fainted.

CHAPTER XV.

THE MONASTERY OF HANGO.

WHEN I awoke, I found myself in my chamber, one of the female domestics watching by my side. My first question was, where was Smerande; I was told she was watching by the side of her dead son; Gregoriska had gone to the Monastery of Hango.

No more thoughts of flight: Kostaki was no more. No more dreams of marriage: Could I espouse a fratricide? Three days passed in listless anxious forebodings: three nights in strange and horrible visions, in which the living gaze of the dead man's eyes were ever visible. On the third day Kostaki's funeral was to take place. In the morning Smerande sent up to my chamber a complete suit of widow's apparel. I dressed myself and went into the chapel. As I crossed the threshold, Smerande, whom I had not seen since the fatal evening, met me. She seemed like the very personification of grief. With a slow, languid movement, she placed her cold lips upon my brow, and in a voice which seemed from its unearthly tone to come from the grave, she pronounced the habitual words: "Kostaki loves you." Language cannot describe to you the effect produced on my shattered nerves by these few words. The protestation of love made in the present and not in the past tense— as if the dead man's love had outlived life itself, seemed not the effect of accident, but of a strange ordination. A sensation came over my mind as if I had indeed been espoused to Kostaki—not the affianced of his brother. The mourning habiliments which encircled me seemed like a shroud: and I was, in spite of my own senses, fascinated with terror.

I looked round for Gregoriska: he was resting against a column, pale and motionless, with up- lifted eyes and clasped hands. I do not know that he saw me.

The monks of the monastery of Hango sur- rounded the corpse, chaunting the psalms of the Greek ritual for the dead in tones sometimes harmonious, but more often monotonous and harsh. I essayed to pray, but the prayer died away on my lips; owing to the excitation of my nervous system I was completely enervated, and I could scarce shake off the impression that I was assisting rather at a consistory of demons than a concourse of priests.

I made a movement to follow the corpse, as they lifted it from the bier, but my feebleness overcame me. I felt my limbs giving way under me, and was obliged to cling to the door to pre- vent my falling. Smerande came towards me, and made a sign to Gregoriska to approach. He obeyed; when his mother addressed him in a few words.

"My mother has ordered me to give you, word for word, the interpretation of what she says to myself," he said, turning to me.

Smerande spoke for a few moments in a tone of deep, sorrowful feeling. When she had ceased speaking, Gregoriska, turning to me, and speak- ing in French, said:—

"Listen to my mother's words; they are these: You weep for my son, Hedwige; you love him, do you not? My heart thanks you for those tears of love. From this day you become my daughter—as if my son Kostaki had been your husband. Let our tears fall freely for the dead—it is a duty we owe to him who is no more; afterwards we will demean ourselves with that calm dignity which belongs to me as *his* mother—to you as *his* betrothed. From this day you have a country, a mother, and relatives. You will now re-enter that home, as the widow of my murdered boy. For myself, I go to follow my son to his last resting-place; on my return, I shall shut myself up with my sorrows and my despair—you see me no more till I have con- quered them; for conquer them I must. I have duties to perform which demand that I live."

My tears were the only response to the appeal thus made to me by the bereaved mother.

I was conducted to my chamber: the proces- sion departed from the chapel.

I have spoken to you of the depressing in- fluence which these fatal events had on my nervous system—above all I was haunted by that awful death-stare of the deceased Kostaki. On this night I felt overwhelmed with a vague horror: and the intensity of my feelings seemed to become heightened as the evening drew on. About nine o'clock I became a prey to a new sensation. Preceded by an indefinable anxiety, I felt myself overpowered by an irresistible drowsiness, accompanied by an oppressive pain at my heart, and a dimness of vision. I fell on my bed, powerless, but not insensible ; motionless, but still keenly susceptible to everything that passed around me.

I heard a step approach my door : the door opened ; I saw nothing—heard nothing farther : but felt a sharp painful sensation in my neck. A moment after I fell into a profound lethargy : and recollect nothing until I awoke about midnight : my lamp was still burning. I essayed to rise from the bed, but my weakness, which seemed to have doubly increased, prevented me. Feeling the same acute pain in my neck, I summoned all my energies, and dragged myself, holding on by the wall, to my mirror. I could see nothing on my neck except a small fresh punctured mark, just such as might have resulted from the prick of a pin. I attributed it to the bite of some insect ; and, worn out with fatigue and weakness, I threw myself again on the bed, and slept till morning.

I awoke with a sense of utter prostration, such as I never before recollect, except on one occasion after I had been bled. After two or three attempts, I succeeded in rising. On going to my glass, I was horror-struck at the unnatural pallor of my countenance: it seemed as if not a particle of blood remained in my system ; and throughout the day I experienced an invincible langour, and craving for rest.

A second night followed, and I experienced the same sensations: only on awaking I felt a greater degree of lassitude, and, if possible, my pallor had even become more strikingly visible.

I resolved to quit the chamber, and go down stairs to Smerande, feeble as I was : when a servant entered my room, and announced Gregoriska, who followed immediately behind her.

I made an attempt to rise from my seat—but it was futile.

He uttered a cry of astonishment when he saw me, and evinced a wish to embrace me, but stopped as he saw my hands extended to prevent this demonstration of affection.

"Why have you come here ?" I demanded of him.

"Alas !" replied he, "I have come to bid you adieu. I have come to tell you that I am about to quit the world, which, with the loss of you and your love, is to me insupportable. I am about to retire to the Monastery of Hango."

"If I am lost to you, Gregoriska, my love is not. Alas ! I love you ever—and God only knows how dearly—how truly. My greatest grief is, that this love, from henceforth, appears to me a crime."

"Then may I hope for your prayers, Hedwige ?"

"Yes : for the little time I am in the world."

"My God ! what has then happened ? Why are you so deadly pale ?"

"I trust that God has taken pity on me, and is about to take me to himself."

Gregoriska seated himself by my side : he took my hand, for I had no power to resist him, and looking at me fixedly, he said :

"Yours is not a natural pallor, my Hedwige : what is the cause of it ?"

"If I tell you, Gregoriska, you will think that I am silly."

"No—no, Hedwige. Tell me, I entreat you. We are in a country which resembles no other : we are of a family which, in its terrible history, is unequalled. Tell me all, I beg of you."

I did tell him all. I told him of the strange hallucination by which I was beset ; of the regularity in its hour of approach ; of the vague terror which nightly overwhelmed my faculties. I recounted to him the sensation of weariness with which I was nightly afflicted ; the phenomena of the approaching step and opening door ; the sharp poignant anguish which followed the appearances I had described—the languor and pallor which succeeded.

I had believed, when I commenced my tale of sorrow, that Gregoriska would have thought the whole affair merely the natural effects of low spirits and deep sorrow ; and it was with some timidity that I narrated these circumstances. To my surprise, he listened anxiously and attentively, and after a pause of some minutes, during which he seemed absorbed in deep reflection, he said—

"You say your first sensations of fear and terror come on you at a particular hour ?"

"Yes ; and the feeling of drowsiness, in spite of all my exertions to resist it."

"And you believe your door is opened ?"

"Yes, although I know it is locked and barred."

"Immediately afterwards you feel an acute pain in your neck ?"

"Yes : and a mark is left on the place."

"Would you allow me to see the mark ?"

I pointed out the spot on my neck, which he examined attentively.

"Hedwige," said he, "have you confidence in me ?"

"What do you wish ?" I asked.

"Can you believe my word ?"

"As I believe in the Holy Gospels," I answered.

"It is well. Then, on my word of honour, Hedwige, you have not eight hours to live, if you will not consent to do, this day, what I request of you."

"And if I consent ?"

"I may, perhaps, save you."

"Perhaps !"

He was silent.

"Whatever may be the result, Gregoriska, I will be guided by you," I replied.

"Listen to me, Hedwige ; but, above all, do not let your fears overcome you. In our country, as well as in Hungary and Moldavia, we have a tradition."

I was terror-struck as I recalled to my mind the traditions of my own country.

"Ah !" said he, "you know to what I allude.

"Yes. I have seen an instance in Poland, of persons subjected to this horrid fatality."

"You allude to vampirism, do you not ?"

"I do. I recollect, in my childhood, seeing disinterred, in the grave yard of a village belonging to my father, forty persons who had died within five days of each other—no one knowing the precise disease of which they died. Twenty-seven of these corpses presented every sign of vampirism—the fresh appearance, the florid

The ride to Hango.—*Page* 84.

countenance, the lifelike aspect : the others were said to be their victims."

"And how was the village delivered from this calamity ?"

"By driving a stake through the hearts and burning the corpses inhabited by the demons."

"Yes : that is the ordinary means ; but, with us, more is required. In order to deliver you from this phantom, I must first know it—and, by heaven, I will know—yes, even though I struggle with it bodily—whatever it be."

"Oh, Gregoriska," cried I, in affright.

"I have said it ; and I repeat it. But it is necessary, in order to put an end to this terrible state of things, that you consent to all that I require of you."

"Say on," I replied.

"Hold yourself ready to go forth from your chamber at seven o'clock: at that hour go below to the chapel—go alone—you will overcome your weakness. Hedwige, you must do this. There we shall receive the nuptual benediction. Will you consent, my own beloved Hedwige ; it is indispensable for your safety that, in the face of God and man, you give me the right to watch by your side. We shall afterwards meet here ; and then come what may, I am prepared."

"Oh, Gregoriska !" I exclaimed, "it will kill you."

"Have no fears, my own dear Hedwige, but give your consent."

"You well know, Gregoriska, that I would do anything you wished me to do."

"To-night, then ?"

"Yes : do on your part all that is necessary, and I will second you to the utmost of my power."

Gregoriska touching the bleeding wound of his brother.—*Page 85.*

He sprang from his seat. In less than a quarter of an hour afterwards I saw Gregoriska riding at full gallop towards the monastery of Hango. I watched his form with beating heart, until a turn in the road hid him from my sight; then I fell on my knees, and in prayer—heartfelt, earnest, and tearful prayer—I spent the time till seven o'clock.

I rose as the clock struck—weak as the dying, pale as the dead. Throwing over my head a thick black veil, I descended the stairs, holding by the wall, and at last reached the chapel without meeting anyone. Gregoriska here awaited me, with Father Bazile, the superior of the monastery. The former carried at his side a sword, blessed and sanctified, a relic bequeathed to the monastery by an old crusader, who had taken a part, with Ville-Hardouin and Baldwin of Flanders, in the taking of Constantinople.

"Hedwige," said Gregoriska to me, striking his hand on the sacred weapon girded on his side, "here is that which shall break the cursed charm that menaces your life. Approach then without fear: behold the holy man who, after receiving my confession, will witness and sanctify our oaths."

The ceremony commenced; never was the sublime ceremony performed in so simple and solemn a manner: no train of bridesmaids—no friends—no gay costume—no bridal wreaths or joyous congratulations: the one solitary priest performed the ceremony and placed the nuptial crown on our heads; dressed in the sombre garb of mourning, we faced the altar, whilst the priest pronounced his blessing in the following words :—

"Go, my children, and God give you strength and courage to fight against the enemy of the human race. Armed with innocence and justice, you will vanquish the demon. Go, and God's blessing be on you."

For the first time, my arm rested on that of Gregoriska, and it seemed indeed that the touch of his strong arm—the contact of his noble heart, gave new life to me. I fully believed that I should triumph, since Gregoriska was with me. We re-entered our chamber.

"Hedwige," said he, "we have no time to lose. Would you rather go to sleep, as usual, and let all be hidden from your view whilst sleeping; or would you rather keep awake and be witness of what passes?"

"Whilst near to thee, Gregoriska, I fear nothing : I will keep awake—I wish to see all."

Gregoriska took from his bosom a small consecrated casket, still moist with holy water, and gave it me :

"Take this box," said he "rest yourself on the bed, repeat your prayers, and await the result without fear. God is with us. Above all, do not release the relique from your grasp —with that, you may master hell itself. Do not call on me ; do not cry out ; but pray, hope, and wait."

I threw myself on the bed : whilst Gregoriska lay down himself behind the raised dais of which I have before spoken, and which cut off a corner of the apartment.

As the usual hour drew near, I felt the same numbness, terror, and icy cold sensation coming over me. I pressed the holy relique to my lips —these sensations disappeared. I heard distinctly the slow and heavy footsteps of some one ascending the staircase and approaching the door of my room. It opened slowly and noiselessly, as if pushed by some supernatural power.

It was then I saw Kostaki—just as I had seen him lying on the litter ; his long black hair, dabbled with blood, hanging over his shoulders ; he was drest in his usual costume, but the front of his vest was open, showing a bloody wound in his breast. Everything in his appearance bespoke death—the ashy grey paleness of the face, the sunken cheek, the rigid muscle—all was of the grave—save the eyes, the burning glances of which outrivalled in intensity even life itself.

Strange as it may appear, instead of feeling weakness at this sight, I felt an increased strength and courage : at the first step the phantom made towards me, I looked it full in the face, and held forth the relic in my hand.

In spite of its evident resolves to reach me, a superior power arrested its footsteps.

"Ah!" muttered the phantom, "she is not asleep—she knows all."

Though speaking in an unknown language, I felt the meaning of what it said.

We were thus face to face, eye to eye, when Gregoriska advanced from behind the dais, holding the sacred sword in his hand. Making the sign of the cross with his left hand, he held the sword pointed at the phantom's breast in his right. With a horrible laugh the phantom drew a sabre which it wore at its side ; but no

sooner did the holy blade touch the weapon of Kostaki, than his arm fell powerless at his side, and he uttered a cry of despair.

"What do you here?" asked Kostaki of his brother.

"In the name of the living God," said Gregoriska, "I adjure you to answer me."

"Speak!" howled the phantom, grinding its teeth.

"Was it I who waylaid you."

"No!"

"Did I attack you?"

"No!"

"Did I wound you?"

"No!"

"You threw yourself on my sword. So, in the eyes of God and man, I am innocent of your blood, and free from the guilt of fratricide. Yours then, is not a mission from Heaven to warn the guilty, but from hell to injure the innocent. To the grave, from whence you have come, you must again return."

"With her, I will go!" cried Kostaki, making an immense effort to gain a hold of me.

"You return alone. That woman is my wife," exclaimed Gregoriska, at the same time the point of the consecrated sword touched the yet bleeding wound of his brother.

With a yell of rage, as if hot iron had touched him, Kostaki retreated. Gregoriska advanced. Thus, the living eyes fixed on those of the dead, the steel pointed at his brother's breast, did they continue, the phantom Kostaki to retreat, the living Gregoriska to advance. Step by step continued this slow and solemn death-march— the spectre retreating before the sacred blade : not a word was spoken ;—the chateau was abandoned—the fields were gained—the forest entered and passed through—the mountain paths threaded and cleared, until they stood face to face beside the open tomb of the Brankovans.

Aided by a supernal power, I had sprung from the bed, and involuntarily followed the brothers in their midnight march—no obstacles seemed to intervene, but it was as if a road had opened for us ; the hilly devious ground became under our feet level and straight ; torrents were dried up ; trees stood aside ; rocks removed themselves at our approach—overhead the sky appeared as if a huge canopy of black crape had been drawn betwixt it and the earth : and as I followed my husband in the awful encounter, I saw nothing but the burning glances of the vampire eyes.

At the side of the grave Gregoriska stopped, and addressing the phantom, said :

"Kostaki, there is yet hope for thee, and who knows but that heaven may pardon thee, if thou repentest. Promise me that thou wilt re-enter thy grave—that thou wilt not again break its bonds—and that the unholy vow thou hast registered shall be withdrawn."

"No!" was the answer.

"Say thou repentest?"

"No!"

"For the last time I ask thee!"

"No!"

"Then call to Satan for aid, as I now call upon God to help me ; and thou wilt see to whom will be vouchsafed the victory."

The cries of the combatants met my ear simultaneously: the swords were again crossed.

Kostaki, with an unearthly cry, fell—the sword had pierced his heart, and nailed him, as it were, to his grave.

I ran forward, as I saw Gregoriska reel, and caught him in my arms.

"Are you wounded?" I asked, in anxious tones.

"No," he answered, "but in such a duel as this, it is not the wound which kills—it is the struggle. I have fought with the dead—I therefore belong no more to the living."

"Dearest, come away ; and far from this, all will yet be well."

"No ?" he replied : "There is my grave. But we lose time, Hedwige. Take a portion of that blood-saturated earth, and apply it to the wound in your neck : it is the only means of preserving you from the fatal effects of this horrible and unholy love : Do this, and live, for my sake, Hedwige ?"

Tremblingly I stooped down, and applied the horrid plaster as he had directed.

"Now, my adored Hedwige," said Gregoriska, in a feeble kusky voice "Listen attentively to my last wishes. Quit this country as quickly as possible : distance is thy only security. Father Bazile has received my last wishes with respect to yourself, and he will faithfully fulfil them. Hedwige, one kiss?—the last—the first—the only one ! Adieu ! I die."

As he uttered these words he fell on the earth by the side of his brother's corse.

I have often wondered that, in the midst of this graveyard, by this side of the open grave, the two corpses lying before my eyes,—that I did not go mad : but, as I have said, I believe that God enable me to support myself under these awful circumstances, in order to bear testimony to what I was not only an eye witness of, but an actor in. I looked around for help ; suddenly the doors of the monastery opened, and Father Bazile, at the head of his confraternity, appeared with lights, and took charge of the bodies.

Smerande, as soon as she heard of this accession of woe, wished to see me. She came to me at the monastery, and heard from my own lips the details I have related to you. No sign of astonishment, no trace of fear escaped her, whilst I narrated my history.

"Hedwige," said she, after a moment's silence, "strange as these things may appear to you, I am fully assured that they are true. There is a curse on the race of Brankovan, even to the third and fourth generation, for in their rage they slew a holy man of God. But happily the term of the ban is expired—for though wife, you are a virgin, and in me the race becomes extinct. If my son has left you a million sterling, take it, it is yours. After my death, with the exception of a few trifling bequests, my fortune will be yours. Now follow to the very letter the advice of your husband. Retire quickly to a country wherein God does not permit such terrible scenes to occur. I wish for no one to weep with me for the loss of my children. Farewell ! make no enquiries after me—for my future belongs only to God and my own heart."

Embracing me, as was her custom, she departed to shut herself up in the lonely castle of Brankovan.

Within a few hours I was on the road to France. As Gregoriska had prophesied, I experienced no more nightly visitations ; my health was re-established ; and I have no trace of the sad events I have recorded except the pallor which you see, and which is said to be the effect produced in the countenance of every one who has been the subject of THE VAMPIRE'S KISS.

————

The lady ceased her narrative. The midnight hour had struck ; and I doubt if the strongest-minded in the company heard its tones without a shudder.

It was time to retire ; and we took our leave of M. Ledru.

In less than a year afterwards, I heard of the death of this excellent man : and it is with no small emotion that I pay a tribute of respect to a good citizen, a learned, and above all, an honest man.

I never returned to Fontenoy-aux-Roses, but the remembrance of this visit to it made such a profound impression on my mind, that I have thought the narratives I there heard might possibly have some interest for my readers : I have thus collected them in one series—under the title of the "Seven Mysteries."

The Death of Gregoriska.—*Page* 87.

W. S. Johnson, "Nassau Steam Press," 60, St. Martin's Lane, Charing Cross.

Lightning Source UK Ltd.
Milton Keynes UK
UKHW031840021222
413117UK00005B/164